Planet Two-Faced

ALSO BY THE AUTHOR

The Itsy Bitsy Family
The Roof Tops
The Alphabets and Friends
The Dream Maker
From Virgin Stream
The Sassenach from Ireland
Board Game
Marry- Go- Round

Planet Two-Faced

Robert Fallon

Matador
9 Priory Business Park,
Wistow Road, Kibworth Beauchamp,
Leicestershire. LE8 0RX
Tel: 0116 279 2299
Email: books@troubador.co.uk
Web: www.troubador.co.uk/matador
Twitter: @matadorbooks

ISBN 978 1785893 704
British Library Cataloguing in Publication Data.
A catalogue record for this book is available from the British Library.

Printed and bound by CPI Group (UK) Ltd, Croydon, CR0 4YY
Typeset in 11pt Palatino by Troubador Publishing Ltd, Leicester, UK

Matador is an imprint of Troubador Publishing Ltd

MIX
Paper from
responsible sources
FSC
www.fsc.org
FSC® C013604

To Elizabeth Dodson & Constance Boxall
Thanks for friendship support and goodybags

To Andrew Dodson & John Morrison
For books promotion, activities and the ALCS and
DACS

CONTENTS

ABOUT THE AUTHOR

The author was born in Lochore, a mining village in Fife, Scotland. The family moved to Leicestershire in England when he was twelve years of age. After a basic education and a broken Painting and Decorating Apprenticeship, he joined the Armed Forces aged seventeen for a short term as a regular. Spent the rest of his working life as a skilled machines operative in several factories. Serious writing came late in life after a very bitter divorce. He enjoys the freedom of writing for all age groups as a hobby.

He is an award-winning poet in a hard-backed book of poetry titled "MODERN TIMES".

He is a member of ALCS and DACS. Collecting societies for authors and visual artists.

PREDICTIONS BY THE AUTHOR

In the 'DREAM MAKER' book written in 2005 and published in 2007 he finds the skeleton of King Richard the Third and predicts a museum will open in Leicester. In the 'SASSENACH FROM IRELAND' published in 2012 he predicts a change of government by 2025, Supermarket space let and railways in big trouble. Although 2025 was written tongue-in –cheek, some of the predictions are already taking shape.

There are a scattering of connected snippets and relevant material to the stories and modern-style poetry in this book, from the previous publications.

DEMOCRASY

We are privileged to live in a country where freedom of speech is allowed. The phone hacking scandal by the Murdock newspaper group put this right in jeopardy. The saying 'It is not what you know but who you know' comes to mind when thinking back on those events. Most of the top players in that deplorable episode escaped with no punishment. With many Members of Parliament angry at journalists reports on their own greed, arrogance and hypocrasy over their fraudulent expenses claims, our freedom of speech was in danger of becoming paper thin.

If those in power gradually silence the newspapers out of existence our days as a democrasy are numbered.

The fact that Members of Parliament still address themselves as honourable members is beyond belief. Their eating of some humble pie may have helped the general public forget the now unforgettable.

THE MILLENIUM BUG

Coughing and sneezing it appeared in our midst as fireworks, costing millions at taxpayers expense, were lit and the Thames on fire was promised we Wonderland Brits. Bug's body was made of a green ball of slime with protruding black eyes above a glowing red snout and antenna that quivered as it begged, 'Help me out!'. It had been around the world spreading germs then interfered with our systems until we shivered and threw up, with evil intent Bug struck at the pounds until they withered away ounce by ounce. It then weakened disabled each inch, foot and yard until, with the threat of being locked up, strange foreign measurements took over our land. Brits fishermen it reeled in on a tight quota line, with foreign detachment it netted them all, to make them housebound on sick pay or the dole. In desperation some turned to crime but they were soon tagged or sent to jail with a fine.

A continental named Euro with marriage in mind came to Wonderland Britain in search of a bride, he bumped into Bug who gave him the flu, now he's weak at the knees with his plans all askew. A Mr. Sleaze and wife Mandy tried in vain to miss

Bug by hiding in Harrods, disguised as two mugs. In France Bug had listened to what every working Brit knew, the continental advice sent his snout glowing red hot. 'Make your way across the channel by whatever way you can for there lies the land of Wonderland Brits who would surrender their all to make him real fit with housing, social benefits and welfare state aid. Parliament, the Queen or gallery called Tate, Brits would even give Spice Girls to make him feel great.'

Bug made it to London where the streets were gold paved laden with cheap booze and thousands of cigarettes taken from the lorry he hid in at Calais, he sold them to Brits without the 'over the top' tax. Printed on the packaging it stated quite plainly, 'Made in London' for export only by land, air or sea. Social Services contacted Bug to give shelter and food, advised it on form filling to make life good.

Feeling real settled as it spread coughs and sneezes with Wonderland Brits it felt quite at ease. Bug then made its way to a tent called The Dome, his antenna had zoomed in on it as he started to roam. He queued up for hours as people were told the body inside was a sight to behold.

Alas, Bug was told at the head of the queue, there is no entry for a Bug such as you. To the National Health Service he was given a note, a full body change for free could be sought. The Brits searched high and low for an intensive care bed where Bug could lay its bug ridden head. Nowhere in Wonderland was there one to be found, only refrigerated lorries with stiff bodies inside.

With taxpayer's money from young and old, back to France the Do Gooders transported this thing. Although delayed there by lorry and farmers blockades in a ward next empty corridors Bug finally stayed, while top surgeons spent months on Bug's body remake. The generous Brits wished him good health, Bug thought what a soft touch, they are really swell. There is no doubt about it Bug will be back to the Wonderland Brits with their Santa-sized hearts. Bug came as a warning to one and all, look after your roots or head for a fall.

EUROPEAN UNION CHAOS

Through mindless incompetence and lack of common sense or forethought, this one size fits all institution is now an ever expanding danger zone. The mix of an avalanche of refugees, migrants and terrorists marching into Europe was on the cards for months before it built up in momentum. If these are the people we have to rely on for our well being and survival, God help us.

THE EU IS NOT JUST FRAYING AT THE EDGES BUT BURSTING AT THE SEAMS.

The British working class are sick to death of our cowardly politicians, civil servants, bankers, money laundering corporations, tax evasion, benefit cheats, cronyism, population explosion to name but a few, of those who put self interest before our culture and country.

They should be very worried about what is taking place at the moment. Why do they think Corbyn in Britain and Trump in America are so popular, against all the odds, with the working classes? Right or wrong they stick to their convictions, so they are trusted. The working class have had their fill of U-turns, lies, deceit and greed.

Meanwhile rich Arabs are buying up the most desirable properties and land in Britain. Fortunes are being spent on the building of magnificent Mosques all over the country for our new arrivals, while our churches become derelict. The future is unfolding in front of our eyes. Are they taking the lead from their Russian counterparts, when their lifestyle in their countries become unsustainable. In the foreseeable future we may be boasting of the most Penthouse refugees of any country.

One is naive and open to all.
The other knows how
to beg and crawl.

THE E-U REFERENDUM

Those with the most to lose if we leave have a
vested interest in staying in. The gravy train
passengers. MEPs. Some large corporations.
Smugglers. Human trafficking. Illegal migrants.
The European Union in its entirety

We in the UK are already beyond the point of no
return as far as saving our culture is concerned.
Have our politicians blanked out of their memories
what our appeasement to Europe has burdened
us with since the 1930s until now. Prime Minister
Chamberlain came back from a knee-bending
visit to Hitler, waving a worthless scrap of paper,
declaring to a relieved and cheering crowd, "peace
in our time." Now David Cameron is leaving a large
environment footprint, as he travels around Europe
like a starving headless chicken desperate for a last
crumb from an overflowing table of unaccountable
bureaucrats. These are specimens of humanity who
owe their freedom to the sacrifice of our nation
when it fought on alone against a ruthless tyrant for
the first two years of World War Two, before the rest
of the world woke up to the reality of a future of
slavery and death.

The gravy on the railway track between Brussels

and Strasbourg is now so thick and greasy, the train glides to and fro without power or stabilisation.

People who believe the EU saved us from a third World War are mistaken. The only thing that stops that tragedy is, sad to say, the nuclear deterrent. The fact is that the EUs rapid expansion to the Russian borders is now the major problem on that subject, plus open betrayed borders.

Stuart Rose, chairman of the stronger in Europe brigade, is a corporate careerist. He declared that those wishing to leave the EU were unpatriotic. An astonishing comment from a lord of the kingdom who, with many of his stature, over many years have let the EU nibble away at our sovereignty and culture. Surrendering our independence to a foreign mismatch who will not be satisfied until they completely dominate our nation. What we have proved over hundreds of years is with the right leadership we are the envy of the World. What we have lacked in and is in short supply is now obvious, no matter which political party you support. A ten Downing Street Cabinet free from cronyism, expenses scandals and addictions. With the dedication, determination and oratory of a wartime Winston Churchill. Or the much maligned greengrocer's daughter, betrayed by her own party. She scorned U-turns which shamed the recent Coalition government and led to the downfall of the Liberal Party and its leader Nick the U-Turner Clegg. A flag waving EU supporter

Germany
2016
January

Angela Merkil

I feel a deep sympathy for the present German nation and their leader. I believe they over-compensated for past history and the misery of the Berlin Wall in their open borders policy to refugees. Their good intentions could and are more than likely to turn into a never-ending nightmare for them and the rest of the EU. For a country that has an enviable record of order and stability from the Second World War when it resurrected itself, common sense deserted them on this occasion.

Although gifted in her chosen profession, Angela Merkil is obviously not well-informed on the sexual frustrations of virile young men. Many thousands turned up on her doorstep. They were from countries where women are segregated and play second fiddle to men. As I thought everybody was aware, for such women to accidentally show a glimpse of bodily flesh to a man, apart from their hubby, they can be severely punished. To come from these places of medieval customs and full body cover-up, our western chicks are a tempting target to these migrants with no family restraining their lust and general behaviour.

She must have been aware that the British Government, in 2015, with lack of thought or proper supervision, trained Libyan forces recruits in England. They ran wild and local females were their main target. Incidents like this get little media coverage. I wonder why?

The New Years Eve shocking migrant behaviour in Germany came as no surprise to many Brits.

POLAND

Poland's Prime Minister said she did not see eye to eye with David Cameron on the issue of delaying our benefits to immigrants. What is her problem? The Polish people here are not spongers and work for their pay, many setting up their own business. She should be more worried about why so many want to come and do something about it. The UK has been draining many countries of their best talent for years, at the expense of our own well-educated youngsters.

On a tour of Poland in 2015 I met a university teacher who was also a tour guide to make ends meet. She stated, "Many of our best and brightest young people are leaving to live in Britain, they are having many children. The ones who stay here are not having children because they cannot afford them."

Sooner or later our governments policies of recruiting from abroad will cause more problems here and backfire big time.

If all EU members paid their nations benefits equal to ours by cutting waste and excesses and expenses at the top, they would deny our Prime Minister his chicken runs.

A German gentleman of some importance was interviewed on British television in January 2016. He seemed to imply that the present young generation had put the past behind them.

I hope they don't, and take lessons of history seriously. The gullible and naïve need constant reminding of the dangers of brainwashing by those with evil intent.

In Britain we now have privileged university students trying to stifle open debate through political correctness and closing up talk shop to those who disagree with their twisted ideology. These people are as dangerous as all our egg-heads who were secret agents for Russia during the cold war. It's a sobering thought that some of these individuals may one day be sitting in the seats of power. But at least they are the enemy we know and hopefully our destiny will be decided by us, without outside interference.

As a nine years old in 1945 my memory of those wartime years is crystal clear. When our nation was united as never before or since and our culture and pride of who we were was never in doubt.

HIDDEN AGENDA?

To my disappointment David Cameron PM, has turned into a replica of Tony Blair PM. He uses the same tactics at Prime Minister Questions Time, spending precious time on important debate, deriding the opposition. He seems obsessed with staying in the European Union, no matter what it costs. His fawning submission to the European bureaucrats is a reminder of Blair's stomach-churning stooge act with President Bush. The PM has announced very early that he will step down from the leadership at the next election. Was there a hidden agenda like the shattered hopes of Tony Blair to be the next President of Europe?

D-DAY

JUNE 6TH 1944

From British Isles this day would die
Proud young men for freedoms cry.
To vanquish tyranny of Nazi Heil,
As Europe it raped, enslaved, defiled.
The allies did Germans much confuse
In dummy bases, machines and news.
With backup strong the Nazis scanned
Beaches not in the battle plan.
Then allied forces made history
Crossed English Channel on this, D-Day.

The sky was filled with drones and shapes
Of airborne armada with much at stake,
Towing large gliders filled with men
To glide inland, disrupt, defend.
The sea alive with ships enmasse
Some floating harbours towing aft
A fuel line under sea
Would sustain attack into Germany.
From Normandy beaches troops stormed ashore
To fight the Nazis to poisoned core.

Many years have gone on by
Their deeds of valour will never die.
The suffering for us was not in vain
We bow our heads, freedom still reigns.
Remember we will the debt that's due
Till unto death we join with you

V E DAY

Church bells rang, gave out the news
Victory was ours in World War Two
People poured into the streets
With hugs and cheers, tears of relief
At last they were free of Nazi Heil
Bombs, bullets, torture, gas chambers vile
Streets were turned from drab to gay
With Union Jacks on proud display
Tables laid out for a feast
Ration books emptied supplied the eats
Okie, koky, Lambeth Walk, singing,
dancing we rejoiced
Blackout over streetlights on
The starting of a bright new dawn
The world owes much to bulldog breed
We gave our best, freedom to keep.

1945
REMEMBER WHEN

Worn out shoes, scratched up knees
A jumper threadbare, stiff in cuff
From umpteen usage from nose and such.
The bite of strap from teachers strict
Red weals of discipline in its grip.
Rupert bear in daily paper
Teaching of a different nature.
Open fields and hills to roam
Safe to let loose on your own,
Following the baker's horse
Garden manure not to be lost.
Cartload of coal dumped in the street
Stacked in back yard before you eat.
Pit clothes soaking in tin bath
After Ma had washed Dad's back.
Stale jam sandwich returned from pit
Eaten with pride
A penny for the pictures
Which were all black and white.
Cleaning fire range with black lead
A must also the front door step.

Queued five hours for bread and meat
Dropped under a bus
Took home in fright now tyred to mush.
Sweets were rationed a quarter a week
But I still have all my front teeth
A bonfire large to celebrate
Returning heroes from the war
In shadowy fringe I kissed and touched
Young Jenny I adored.

MAN IN STITCHES

Harold Parslow take a bow
Stitched all over, inside and out
Shrapnel wounds to nose and head
One toe taken clean from flesh.
Surgeon's knife at stomach aimed
Nevus giving so much pain,
Gallbladder removed, in despair
Hospital becoming a care home.
A battle with cancer tumour
Saw him near the end of tether
Blood clots gave the heart a jolt
Then double hernia took hold.
Hip joints now has had replaced
Profanity utters as patience strays.
Could I be as strong I wonder.
A bookworm with standards high
An education for you and I.

GORBALS MAN

Born in a Glasgow slum
A life of squalor had begun
One toilet on the tenement stair
All who lived there
Had to share.
Foul smelling, overflowing loo
A nightmare for all who used.
Overcrowded, six to a bed
Lucky if you owned a chair
In the days when jobs did not exist.
Each tenement had its tribal gang
Lives were ruled by Razor scars
Or head butt known as Glasgow kiss
So not much difference from then to this.
In this environment humans survived
The blood line not to be denied.
For this mockery of a life
Men for country, gave lives and limbs.

THE PIT PIECE

It was no morsel of great taste
Stale bread with jam that tasted sooty
But it had been where your heroes go
Down the coalmine far below.
The miners saved some for the kids
On Mary Pit road at end of shift.
Pit siren wails in still of night
You wake up mam, who dresses quick.
With her you stand at the pit head
As cage brings up deformed and dead.
No longer will you see dad grin
Holding out pit piece
In vacuumed tin.
On Lochore Meadows now made for pleasure
Ghost with pit piece below forever.

JAM JARS OF HOT TEA

Coal fire burning bright
Tin bath on fire rug ready
Waiting on Gran's miner sons
His uncles Sam and Eddie.
On black-leaded hob
Two jam jars of hot tea
Best china kept for Sundays
That's how it used to be.
Who would win the race
To step into tin bath
Then with a grin
Leave water black
The loser's lot to have.
Uncle Sam's the winner
Gulps his jar of tea
To clear his throat of coal dust
Gargles with great glee.
Pit siren gives it's mournful wail
Disaster down below,
Granny's face goes tense and white
Somehow the worst she knows.
Eddie's jar of tea shudders on the hob
Then with a crash falls to the floor
With no one near to touch.
Sam looking dejected

Wearily gets dressed
Pit clothes he puts in bath to soak
He knows where Eddie rests.
All have now departed earth
Somewhere they wait for him
On Grannies hob he knows there sits
His jam jar of hot tea.

GLOBAL POWERS

It took a supreme and heroic effort, at great cost, hardship and grief to their nations, for the Allied Global Powers to conquer international tyranny in World War 11.

We now have one tin pot Dictator holding the World to ransom. If he had a sliver of decency and humanity in his brain, he would have abdicated years ago. There is no virtue in pounding his people and country into dust.

After all their meetings, junketing and photo shoots, todays powers that be cannot even agree to remove this insanity peacefully.

Global Power is no longer in the hands of people who put the welfare of the World at the top of their agenda. It is now a conglomerate of the powerful, intent on self-interest.

LEICESTER
A MULTI RACIAL CITY

The ordinary person
is not hard to please.
Secure employment
a pleasant environment
places of leisure
peace and contentment
as they age.
Leicester is steeped in history
through centuries in time
a relic from Roman occupation
the Jewry wall in city centre.
King Richard the Third
slept his last night
in city at the Blue Boar Inn.
First free schools for the poor
By Christian benefactors.
Thomas Cook introduced
The package holidays.
Our museums, streets and statues
are much more explicit.
A city of commerce
public transport second to none.
A city council with common sense
found it pays to burden less
one orange bag recycles all
one bin to put weekly rubbish in.

In harmony we multi-racials live
taste buds delight
from world cuisine.
Colourful Indian festivals
are well supported.
Rio style carnivals
refresh the senses
cheers of delight
in streets, from houses.
Our Muslims slowly modernise.
For years young men have camped
at the port of Calais
my opening lines
the dream they carry
English Channel
Life changing barrier
Open borders make no sense,
all we cherish put at risk.

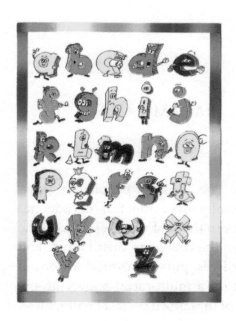

Why the political
correct crept into our
lives.
Read on.

The
Alphabets
and friends

Robert Fallon

RACISM

The tolerance of the British people to mass immigration especially over the last decade has been remarkable. I can think of no other nation who could have handled the change to their culture and disruption to their lives, plus the cynical actions of the elite, hell-bent on a multi-racial society at any cost. With the help of the cursed political correctness, the British public, which already contained in mainly industrial areas, large migrant populations, were subdued into passive silence, black and white, in fear of being accused of being a racist. Any word or object that might upset the sensitive feelings of incoming settlers, was banned or severely criticised by our politically motivated governments and institutions. I could never understand why Indian friends were described as black, when they were more like me, but with the advantage of a suntan. Even our beloved Golliwogs were banned. Through idiotic political correctness like this, plus housing, schooling and benefits policies etc., our political elite succeeded in arousing a simmering anger in a peace-loving silent majority. They were treated as second class citizens by those they voted into power.

My first encounter with the political correct was many years ago, when writing my educating Alphabet book. I went to the Literary Advice Bureau. I was told, if I wanted to have any chance for it being accepted in schools I must change a number of names. There were too many of Anglo-Saxon origin for our multi-racial society. The name Willie would have to be changed, children might think it meant something else. The rhyme 'Mum, Itsy Bitsy works all day, unlike Dad she gets no pay' was classed as sexist. These and other changes were duly made. I thought at the time there was more to this than just the lack of common sense. I am convinced from what has happened since, that this was the beginning of a concentrated attack, through political correctness, on free speech. In my lifetime I've been called many things, including Limey, Jockstrap, Halfpint, Dwarf, Rab, Rabbie, Rob, Wanker and many unprintables. For goodness sake , get a life all you political correct, over-sensitive, sad, humourless people before you wipe the smiles and freedom from the face of the earth. I live in a multi-racial city as a white-faced Jockstrap in England. A Muslim lady knocked on my door in 2005 and asked for my help. I finished up teaching her children and redecorating their home. My book 'THE DREAM MAKER' was based on this family. In 2004 some Indian friends talked me into going to Goa, India instead of Phutec. As I lay on the beach in Goa, the Tsunami hit the beach in Phutec. Thanks guys, I owe you all BIG TIME.

WHERE DO I BELONG?

After spending many months in the multi-racial area where he lived, Robbie decided to treat himself to a Sunday lunch in the village of Anstey, 4 miles from the city centre. As he sat in the crowded restaurant he began to feel ill at ease, something was definitely wrong. Suddenly, it became clear, there was not a black or coloured face to be seen. They were all white-skinned and chattering away in English, it felt like he was in a different country. He felt so out of place that he left his half-eaten meal and drove back to his mixed-up community. What worried him most was why he had felt more at home in Goa, India, than in an English village 4 miles from his home. Was he losing his Identity?

TICKING TIME BOMB

A gathering of over two hundred people in 2015 attended an event titled, "QUIZ A MUSLIM". The panel consisted of six radical Muslims, well known for their extreme political views. By a strange coincidence this event took place during the massacre of innocent civilians in Paris, France by ISIS terrorists and continued throughout the attack. A panel member spoke of a Caliphate in Britain where Muslim laws should be given priority. The main theme of this event was to turn Britain into a Muslim state.

A Muslim Member of Parliament described the event as insensitive and mischievous. What a pathetic response by this so-called honourable member to a serious threat to our national security and democracy.

This panel of the unsatisfied also complained about the British government trying to push British values onto Muslims. The arrogance and abuse of our hospitality by these sanctimonious extremists is beyond civilised understanding. If they are not happy with our way of life and disrespect our culture they should leave our country. The peaceful majority of all creeds and cultures would be happy to cheer them on their departure.

We are now suffering as a nation once again, from the appeasement of our weak-kneed politicians and a justice loaded in favour of the accused by wiggy wonders heading for senility. Out of touch with reality and the well-being of the silent majority. For decades Muslim extremists have been allowed to preach their propaganda on our streets, without fear of reprisal. Their grubby hands should be deprived of all the benefits they receive from our democratic country that they threaten to overturn.

Around the time of the Paris massacre a Muslim woman was secretly filmed, preaching racial hate to women and children in a British recreational hall. If any justice was brought to bear on her, which I doubt, it certainly did not make the headlines in the media.

To top all this we then had the Deputy Prime Minister, Jeremy Corbyn, saying our security forces should not be allowed to shoot to kill armed terrorists on our streets.

It is no surprise that we are regarded as a soft touch Worldwide, from benefits for children who do not live here, to obeying a flawed Human Rights law which stops us deporting foreign scum. We are powerless to deport all the legal and illegal immigrant killers, rapists, child abusers and many others with fraudulent, treasonable and terrorist intent.

At the same time we act quickly, with no compassion or common sense to deport a ninety-two years old lady visiting her daughter, who has overstayed her visa.

One is
anti-austerity.

Wealth accumulation
for two
an
obsession.

THE KINGDOM
OF
BLAIRSPIN

Once upon a time in this democratic Island, there reigned a King Corbyn and Queen Abbot. The King was a descendant of King Foot, who had kicked this Island of prosperity into the red during his short reign. Queen Abbot, who had been in labour for a long painful time, had just given birth to a son. The King wept with joy as he witnessed the birth. He was an ageing agitator, with fixed views which were contrary to the wealth, trappings and privileges which he now enjoyed.

If the royal couple could have foreseen the worldwide suffering that would unfold from this birth, they would have been horrified.

There were many signs that Prince Blairs was of a different nature to his parents. For suckling and grasping he was right-handed and also preferred to sleep on his right side. On reaching puberty he dressed his projection to the right. The King on the other hand, was an out and out leftist, with the Queen's approval.

After an expensive education he turned out to be a charming young man with a winning smile.

His greatest asset was a glib tongue, which would become his trademark.

His popularity on the World stage reached a high during a time of deep mourning on an international scale. The Queen until then had given a lifetime of devoted service to her subjects and country. One really shocking misjudgement of the overwhelming sympathy of the nation at this tragic time, by the Royal entourage, put the whole of the Monarchy at risk, with the almost certain change of lifestyle for all the related and unemployed hangers-on. Prince Blairs sensitive handling of the situation at this critical time, saved the day.

The biggest threat to Royal rule from then on came from the far north and south of the country. In the north the Tartan Clans were dancing the Highland Fling, and waving their Claymores in a threatening manner as they wailed through their bagpipes for Independence. King Corbyn tried, without success, to please them with anti-austerity measures and more self-rule.

The House of Ermine in the south was home to an army of pensioners. They had lived all their lives off the fat of the land. They were now trying to take over power, by dissent. It doesn't take a stretch of the imagination to realise why this sanctuary of easy money, for just turning up, was better known as the House of Cronies and Past Favours. It was now filled to the rafters and had put in a takeover bid for the House of Commoners, which was decaying from age and masonry.

King Corbyn ordered Prince Blairs to find a remedy for the north—south divides. Blairs approached the Palace golf fanatic and international playboy for advice. Andy Fergie and his close family were well-tuned into worldwide connections and gossip, from their busy workload of excessive holidays in high society hot and cold pleasure spots. Andy informed Blairs of a white witch he knew who might be of help. She had arrived recently as another illegal immigrant, hidden in a large pigskin diplomatic bag. She was being sheltered in the Downing Street area of Lundone after escaping from the country of Cameroon, by a bunch of curious Jabbering Gabbies, address unknown. Disguised as an election campaigner for the Raving Loony Party, Blairs searched for her door to door. By a strange coincidence this led to him meeting the love of his life. Cherie Garnet, an early to bedder, answered her doorbell in a flannel nightie, with her hair in steel curlers. It was love at first sight as they gazed at each other in shock and awe. Cherie looked a picture of innocence as she walked up the aisle on the arm of her proud and royalty-loving father, Alf Garnet. Blairs knew at that moment there was no need now to search any further for the services of the white witch. He had wanted her to cast a spell of destruction on the House of Ermine and to silence forever the emotion-inspiring sound, for the Scots Clans, of the bagpipes. Princess Cherie could outmanoeuvre any witch or human being. She had two minor faults, her love of freebies and no-ticket train journeys. He had found his Sindrella.

With her now royal status, Princess Cherie's part-time job in Human Rights became a lot more productive. These Human Rights laws were perforated with many loopholes, making them a never-ending source of wealth for unscrupulous lawyers and a nightmare for victims. Blairspin Judges, unlike many of their species in other Domains, appeared to look personally as well for any loophole in favour of the prosecuted and not the victim. Victims and general public were crying in despair, and clamouring, unheeded, for a Victims Rights Charter without outside interference.

King Corbyn retired from his duties to his subjects when he became seriously unhinged, from a common but fatal illness, known as the Anti-Austerity Syndrome. Prince Blairs and his bride took over the reins of power. Unlimited power brings out in most people a rapid increase in egoism, Blairs and Cherie were no exception.

They became so cocksure of themselves they set about putting the World to right.

The country of Blairspin, against all enemies and conflicts, had always punched above its weight and size. After great sacrifices in lives, limbs and the hardship of two World Wars, the population was struggling to keep their heads above water. At the same time the powers that be appeared to be more interested in international prestige and glory. Giving billions of pounds in money in overseas aid, with no clear indication of how much was being skimmed off before reaching, and after delivery. It seemed ironic to the Blairspin peasants that many of the rulers of those so-called poor countries, were living in luxury and some into enterprises that their own homeland could not afford.

Blairs, his common sense now lost in his self-belief, started his call to arms with a foray into the Balkans. This was reasonably successful, which increased his appetite for war. His ingratiating behaviour when acting like a stooge to an American President during the second Iraq War, was an embarrassment to his countrymen. But their contempt for him was complete when a 'weapons of mass destruction' statement by him proved to be untrue. In the years that followed millions of people would count the cost. Probably the most far-reaching, devastating untruth in the history of mankind.

Prince Blairs reluctantly went into exile in an undemocratic handover to his Chancellor, Crabby Brown. He soon had his sights set on an even more profitable and powerful post. The Presidency of the European Union was now up for grabs. Unfortunately for him, the fact that he was from the isolated country of Blairspin, plus his warmongering and wealth-seeking at every opportunity did him no favours. Having saved Europe from certain German domination through two World Wars, there was a feeling in Blairspin of mixed European emotion towards them, a mix of admiration, jealousy, guilt and fear. Thinking they were doing us a favour, they helped Blairs get a Peace Envoy post in the middle east. This was as startling to the Blairites as the time they banned bent bananas. They must have had no idea of the depth of ill-will towards this man. The howls of derision from Blairspin's angry majority were heard but not recorded.

By this time the bureaucrats of the EU were more, not less, ruling the country of Blairspin and charging its peasants billions of pounds for the privilege.

Meanwhile, Queen Abbot was enjoying her retirement from power. She had more time to spend with her two friends at the BBC. Mick Portillo, who was homeless and lived on trains after being politically sunk in his prime. Neil Andrews, her other close friend, was a BBC presenter with day and night political talk shows.

As the BBC had for some reason been accused of being too left wing, Neil was very careful in getting his questions and answers spot on. This had turned him into a statistics freak. He always had sheets of them at hand to stimulate debate and chit-chat. They were his constant companion and many a drowsy night they would be disturbed under his pillow. The thought of being outsmarted was his ultimate nightmare. His other obsession was having mugs on his shows.

The BBC at this time was fighting for survival in its now prehistoric form. The building itself was in danger of collapse, leaning more and more to the left. The many clusters of chatty news readers, good and bad weather friends, entertainment stars and dancing gigolos were biting their well-manicured nails in anxiety. Even the dreaded word 'ADVERTISE' was being whispered behind closed doors. Luckily there was one expensive scapegoat to give them a little reprieve and maybe time to catch their breath. All the taxpayers favourite sports programmes were being axed or cut to the bone.

Mick Portillo and Queen Abbot had no worries about payment for their nights out. Neil was a generous host with the Midas touch. Mick's passion for multi-coloured jackets was indulged to the full. Queen Abbot was saved the humiliation of feeling through King Corbyn's pockets for welfare donations to educate children. Although the BBC paid their staff mouth-watering salaries they were tight-fisted when it came to paying for trinkets. It was a good job that Neil could afford to pay for mugs and all, from his larger-than-life petty cash.

Prince Blairs and partner had departed on a luxury holiday which they were actually paying for with their own money. No fairy-story ending, but with Chill Plot enquiry ongoing, for glib tongues there were rich pickings.

THE
CHILL PLOT
ENQUIRY

Too hot to handle, passed down the line, hoping
it would fade away with the passage of time. The
most shameful farce in our history, six years and
counting, will it never end, feeding off bereavement
and injured brave men.

A government with integrity would bust a gut to
back-pedal quickly from this cronyism bluff, saving
many years of misery and public disgust.

There was no need for an enquiry at all, or the
gravy train for some political storm. With the World
watching on television, the instigator told the bare-
faced lie that set in motion World upheaval and
untold harm. If justice was served all involved
would be punished, all assets seized to compensate
injured and bereaved. This enquiry was rotten to
the core. Whatever happens, history will judge this
blatant betrayal.

My Love's Like A Red Red Rose

BURNS NIGHT

Your words endure
To lift our hearts
Touch our cheeks with dew
as we address the haggis
and drink to fire in you.
I wish her well
she is a classy lassie
But breaking up
could turn out nasty.

SCOTLAND'S
REFERENDUM

At the Scottish National Party conference on the 15th October 2015, the fanatical members of the independence brigade were hell-bent on a second referendum. Leader Nicola Sturgeon, who I admire for her tenacity and being true to her beliefs, even down to her very smart red outfit, had more common sense. She now knew that the silent majority in Scotland were as canny as herself, when they joined the gathering of the Clans in the SNP. They would not leave the security of the UK, which was pretty stable, until some future date where there was no chance they would plunge into an abyss.

With the dramatic fall in oil prices and the present state of the EU, there must be a lot of her MPs sweating with relief as they sit in wonder in the House of Commons at all the noisy jabbering and rowdy schoolboy behaviour surrounding them.

It is a strange irony that the main driving forces in the SNP are named after fish, the Salmon and the Sturgeon. It must be a constant reminder to them both, that the EU, without scruples, took the guts and all out of the east coast of Scotland fishing industry.

From the Forth Bridge to Aberdeen and beyond.

It is now obvious that this organisation will not give up its goal of independence. But why do they want to remain in the EU, subject to its rules and regulations? This is replacing the Auld Enemy which they manipulate so easily, with a dictatorial, foreign institution, stuck in uniformity. No way could this be called independence. A better description would be political suicide.

I am a proud, born and bred Scot, whose family was jobless and moved to England as migrants in a clapped-out van, six of us in the back with a bucket as a toilet. It was mid-winter 1948. In those days it was a long slow trip over the borders and the Yorkshire moors with frequent breakdowns and snow drift hold-ups. A journey of slight inconvenience compared with the suffering of today's migrants through the EU open borders policy and lack of foresight.

It was a wee bit naughty of the SNP to charge the English students tuition fees and not foreigners. If this had been a case concerning all black or, dare I say it, coloured students, the Human Rights lawyers and the politically correct would have been hammering and knocking down the doors of the Scottish Parliament, bringing their placards and banners, waving writs for racial discrimination.

To save the British public maybe many years of worry before Nicola feels ready to pounce, action by the present English government needs to be taken. I am sure Nicola would be more than happy to be voted out of the United Kingdom. As a last gesture of goodwill the cost of border controls and passports could be shared. Nicola could lay the last stone on a rebuilt Hadrian's Wall.

Bank on him for
the Earth's red glow
as he stokes fires
of hell below.

BANKERS – BAMBOOZLE

I am an eighty years old pensioner, on a working class state pension, with an easy-going nature, until someone makes my blood boil. This has been happening much too often in the last decade. All age groups now have too much crap to deal with in their everyday lives. My former bank are responsible for my efforts to have this latest book published. This bank and its British counterparts have learnt nothing from the catastrophe they brought about in 2008. PPI is just one example of them turning the clock back. The top tier are as arrogant and untouchable as ever. If the law in this country was on a level playing field many would be locked up and the key thrown away. All our futures are, once again, in their grasping hands. It is time for Global Powers – Conglomerates to stop sitting on their hands, grab the reins and stop them once and for all from another stampede to disaster.

They are now changing accounts on a regular basis, sucking clients in, then lowering the Interest Rates a year later. With my latest account with my former bank, if you wanted a little more interest, instead of practically nothing, you had to pay in

£1500 a month and have at least two Direct Debits. This interest which only applied to the first £5000 in your account averaged about £12 a month. If you did not pay in the full amount you were fined £5. My pension was not enough to cover the monthly £1500, but my account was always well over the maximum interest payment. I also had a substantial amount in a Savings Account with the same bank. From my long-winded and compulsory video watch interview they were also aware I had other funds and was no risky Credit Card holder. As this interest was no Bankers Bonus I did no somersaults from sheer joy, but did not quibble about it either. To my surprise I found out later that I was not allowed to transfer money from my Savings Account into my main account by Standing Order. If the Savings Account had been with another bank there would not have been a problem. How daft can you get ? As the main account was well over the maximum interest rate of £5000 I decided to take out the make-up cash each month and then put it back again. This did not gain me any applause either. If readers are as confused as I am, perhaps the shortened version of the letter from the bank and my reply will help clear the haze.

Bank letter. "As you have not been paying in monthly £1500 into your account you have incurred monthly fees. It may be that one of our other accounts would suit you better. Book a review."

My reply. "Dear Sir, regarding your letter of 18th September, thank you for your concern about my

Club Account. I have been a bank customer for 60 years. With the reputation of Banking in disrepute, the constant changing of Current Accounts, with long-winded reviews to promote other products does not improve its image. With paltry Interest Rates, including ISAs, like many others I prefer to invest my money in more profitable ventures. My Club Account is in credit at around £7000. Having a sense of humour and some common sense, I find the detail in my Club Account amusing, but annoying and time-wasting. I visit my bank most months to take out £400, then put it back in again to make up my £1500 so I do not get fined a measly £5. How daft can it get when I already have around £2000 over the £5000 higher interest limit in the account. Due to my literary travels I sometimes miss my bank visit and lose £5. I have never complained, but being Scottish born and bred this gives me palpitations and a slow recovery, which is normal in an ageing wrinkly. The Banking System will never regain the public trust until it starts operating with common sense and cuts out the culture of greed at the top.

You may view my enclosed book with interest or dismay. My books have been viewed by the PM, the former President of Croatia, the Lady in the White House in Washington DC and the Ambassadors in the American and Russian Embassies in London. Those who replied were complimentary."

For some strange reason after I sent my reply I received two phone calls pleading with me to make a complaint.

ON THE BRIGHT SIDE

There is a bank from a hotter climate
with a much warmer disposition
who are gaining clients with a more
open hand rather than a tight fist
from their British rivals.
With shorter reviews, a simpler system
and much more rewarding interest.

With the rapid advance of
technology our lives appear to get
more instead of less, stressful. We
spend more time than ever
ploughing through piles of junk
mail, charity appeals and cold calls
from International rip-off merchants
and scammers searching for the
vulnerable for easy pickings. Open
borders are bad enough, but we are
now under constant attack in our
own homes.

It fills one with nostalgia for the
days of the Bank Book, no computer
breakdowns, a friendly Copper on
the streets, and an old-fashioned
trustworthy Banker in every Town
and Village.

America
can be proud.
No stain on
character
to be found.

OPEN LETTER TO PRESIDENT OBAMA

President Obama
The White House
Washington DC
From the UK
March 2009

Dear Sir,

You had our deep sympathy when you walked into the White House to face the most appalling legacy left to any American President in recorded history. Events were reaching boiling point when President Bush escaped out of the White House back door. On the oval desk no doubt, was evidence of his indiscretions, mistakes and maybe more. Two on-going conflicts he left you, terrorist cells world wide. To top it all a recession from a Global meltdown that started on your doorstep and might make furrows in your brow.

Are bankers in the USA and United Kingdom living in a fairy wonderland?

They bankrupted their businesses with risky deals using clients cash, to award themselves bonuses of unbelievable size. Then had the nerve to dig into government hand-outs of taxpayers hard-earned tax. In Britain we wonder if our politicians are treading the same path. With generations of sleaze stuck to their shoes and devious bending of Parliaments rules, making a hidden income from family-employed staff and second homes not used. Brazen-faced they then declare that they have done no wrong. We have elected Peers filling their well-fed faces with question scams in the House of Lords. Now in this recession, with millions out of work, some of our politicians have the audacity to ask for a massive pay rise, now rule-bending found out. No doubt this is to cover money they might lose from fiddling from the National purse if there is a tightening of the rules.

The general opinion of the public is politicians with guilt complexes are afraid to take the money men to court, in case, for their own devious ways, they might yet have a price to pay. If the honest men and women at the heart of power don't soon take a stand against widespread corruption in their midst, national rebellions are more of a certainty than a passing chance.
Some humble advice, Sir, that may ease the

stress of your position. Don't try to force American idealism down the throats of other nations. Many of your predecessors did, with tragic consequence. Vietnam is a prime example that President Bush should have heeded. After many years of anguish, death and destruction, communism won the day with America's embarrassing withdrawal. Now without any idealistic help Vietnam is more democratic. The time has gone when any country can police or rule the world. Try to save the planet from its fate as human beings its resources rape...

AMERICAN PRESIDENTS

They would like to be remembered
For their work as head of state
But some go down in history
For words or fibs from oval office.
President Truman's angry outburst
'If you can't stand the heat get out of
the kitchen,'
When all around him got cold feet.
President Nixon's infamy, from one
word WATERGATE
Forced him to resign
He could have left the White House
As a great statesman
Dialogue with China he had just begun.
President Bush went to war
Assuming that Saddam
Had weapons of mass destruction
With his British shadow
Talked Nations into conflict.
President Clinton in office
Served with distinction
Until he announced with a straight face
'I did not have sex with that woman'
Not impeached but in disgrace.

THE BIG THREE

After the chaos of World War Two
At Yalta in the Ukraine a meeting took place
For the big three to carve up Europe.
Questions are still on our lips
About all the suffering that came from this.
Stalin promised in Eastern States, Democracy
he would Decree.
Why did America and Britain trust the
Russian Dictator
When knowing of his ruthless nature?
Should Roosevelt have been there, ill in his
wheelchair
With just three months to live?
Was Churchill weary in his mind from
fighting Hitler and Japan?
From signed agreement Europe was split
For decades millions suffered from it.
From behind barbed wire and concrete walls
Slaves to tyranny arose en masse
When the Berlin Wall was breached
The Big Three at last were in retreat.

NINE – ELEVEN
SEPTEMBER HORROR

They stood in twin splendour
Monuments to human ingenuity
Shimmering in the morning haze
Above the urban sprawl.
Suicidal Jihad fanatics
Flew into the Towers that day
The world watched in disbelief
As the second Tower was struck
Then both crumbled into dust,
Millions would count the cost.
No written words of any creed
Should by acts like this be blasphemed
Or those seeking religious direction
Be cloned by adult seed.
The aftermath brings misery
As eye to eye confronts
Terror with eternal goal
To jaws of hell is linked.

HASTING'S CUT OFF

California was their goal
From every country they did roll.
Hundreds of miles by wagon train
To end up eaten or insane.
Hasting's short cut was not planned
A route untrodden by this man.
If they had taken longer route
Would not have frozen in their boots
With safety just one ridge to climb
From mountain blizzard they took cover.
Wagons sunk in sea of salt
In Utah had held them up.
Oxen killed by Indian arrows
Those left gorged to bone and marrow.
Some did eat their next of kin
Flesh, heart and liver kept life within.
To the Garden of Eden a few survived
What price to pay to stay alive.
If you're named Donner or a Reid
Remember suffering of former creed.

SURVIVAL

America, land of the dream
Haven for so many gene,
With the world in turmoil to the core
Salvation stems from White House door.
Dark shadows in power mad heads
Tears of blood of innocent shed.
In withered skin with jutting bones
From drought and genocide millions roam.
Religious dogma stalks the soul
With bomb or bullet terrorists call.
Pollution saps Mother Nature's strength
As day by day she chokes on stench.
We lay a shroud over tree and bloom
Through ozone hole watch sun or moon.
Are we so primitively destructively insane
That from our source life blood we drain.
To save all species from extinct
In united state turn back from brink.

THE ENVIRONMENT

As we are continually reminded by our elite, the environment is in a mess. With egoistic, sleaze-ridden Politicians, Dictators and Despots, lavishly fed, pampered, protected and on an endless gravy train, the future for us all looks bleak. The authoritarian rule of Communism, the Taliban and religious zealots of all creeds is also not the answer. There must be found a newer, greener, middle ground that is fairer to all. Or are we to be reeled into oblivion by words that have been twisted through the years, out of all recognition, from books written in the dark ages, and the John Lewis list mentality of our elite.

GREENPEACE

When environment disaster
Hits earth or sea
These dedicated few
Turn up to toil.
Their activities sometimes
Cause a great outcry
From Governments
That they upset.
An inspiring battle
They also fight
For creatures other
Than Mankind.

HUMANS

With bounty gifted
Brain and health
But basic instinct
To kill self.
From bullet, torture
And the bomb
Exudes a melancholy form.
No plague of locusts
In pursuit
Destructs the earth
As does man's boots.

THE BRINK

Ignorance, Intolerance
Lies deep in human race
As with a will it sets about
Destruction of the land.
By billions spawn the human throng
To scrape earth bare, night and dawn
While Granny Smith contracts with glee
From science-induced fertility.
As earth decays a ray of hope
With water found on Mars
The Universe in terror waits
Watches with great awe
Our giant leap into space
Other Worlds to destroy.

THE SEEKERS

In bowls of earth
Dark tremors of the deep
Mankind in search
Not yet complete.
To suck into his treasure chest
All nature bestows
In trust to let.
Voracious the appetite of man
As into throat
The spoils he rams.

ACID

It can be good or harmful
For us all it has some pull
A substance which is much in use
In little pill can turn brain loose.
If around the body lapped
Will eat the flesh from front to back.
As amino acid it is known
To help the hair, head to adorn.
In vinegar it gives the food
A flavour mouth likes to include.
Acid Drops are bottle sweets
To refresh taste buds hard to beat.
As man-made rain it rots the trees
Nature finds it hard to please.
With stomach pain
Or to the chest
With burns it canes
If married to an acid tongue
A life of torment has begun.

SAND

It comes in many a different hue
With uses that are far from few
As on a beach you soak up sun
A golden stretch to lay at leisure.
Children mix it with sea water
Into a castle it can alter.
Three to one mix with cement
Changes into a concrete.
All sort of glass from sand made
Some with names to be engraved.
Poured into canvas bags
Helps keep floodwater at bay.
With it in sandpit kids can play
When far away from the seashore.
Gives smooth texture to the wood
As sandpaper rubbed on crude.
Around the world large quantities lie
How long will this be so?
With man about
Might shrink or grow.

SUMMER

It's come again
Though took long time
Now feeds the fruits
Of root and vine.
White waxed skin
To pink will go
If sun too much
Red face can glow.
Use the sun cream
One and all
For cancer screen
From ozone hole.

HERITAGE

From roots entrenched
In healthy soil
Thrusts stem for vine,
To flourish forth,
The fruit and scent
Of living bloom,
By sun enriched
Though warmth of noon,
With rain to feed
The roots below
Mankind's fulfilment
If nurtured so.

WORKING TOGETHER

Toiling in harmony all as one
For fuller life to be won.
Offering to others a helping hand
Instead of hoarding what we can.
A little time to sacrifice
For those downtrodden in our eyes,
Richer in spirit we can be
By showing some charity.
Like most of us I've done some wrong
As no saint was I born,
But I, like you, can start afresh
By giving more while taking less.

THE BIG BANG THEORY

The following theory, like all others on this subject of our existence, is questionable. But Big Bangs have been the norm, since life began on this Planet. This of course includes the weapons of mass destruction brought upon us by civilisation.

Our Planet was formed by the debris and matter from a vast explosion in space. The cause has been lost in the history of time, bur scientific knowledge of this Big Bang now exists.

For one hundred and fifty million years Dinosaurs roamed the Planet Earth. They fed mostly off their own kind, or by nature evolved to be vegetarian, with very long trunk-like necks, ideal for eating tree-top vegetation. As we know, their body weight and size was amazing.

Their extinction began from another Big Bang, when an asteroid hit Earth. The force of it's explosion changed the climate on Earth. All kinds of plant and tree life withered, then died. With the food chain broken, it was just a matter of time before the skeletons of the Dinosaurs lay, scattered or in large numbers, for us now to survey. Only the most primitive and tiny life forms somehow survived.

It took millions of years for the Planet to recover, more or less from scratch. Ninety-five million years after the Dinosaurs extinction, our DNA, in life form unknown, generated, from DNA stored in particles of matter from the two "Big Bangs".

In a wonderland of seashores, oceans, landscapes and mountains to climb, with fresh air to breathe, our lives began. With a Sun, Moon and seasons, all life forms to possess. It is a miracle of all miracles, that all of these elements fell into line, to give the opportunity to our kind of living in time.

Contentment was never a strong human trait, from Caveman with club and spear, to the destructive force that we now are today. As cultivation of land and humans spread, so did greed, power and envy and blood that ran red. Now the most intelligent species to have walked on this earth, but in varying degrees we are all flawed. As well as the flaws mentioned above, our brains are now overloaded, ready to burst.. With technology increasing at a frightening pace, human emotions tortured through our extremes, thoughts of environmental disaster and an obsession with life after death running wild in our heads.

Billions are spent searching the Universe for a twin of the Planet that we have. While we neglect and destroy each other and poison the air that we breathe.

A COMEDY OF POLITICS
2011

Jaws Brown had started his working life with good intentions, in the manufacturing industry, but with no job security and rip-off pension schemes, he could only see a bleak future ahead of him. A non –productive job in the government, or with the council was the answer, with more job security and inflation-proof pension. The trouble was, most of the population had come to this conclusion. Also, hordes of legal and illegal immigrants were having to be found secure employment first, to supplement free social benefits they had not contributed to. Brown took exception to this and decided with many more to milk the benefit system. He was living a life of luxury, fiddling with large sums of money, when greed and ego got the better of him, number ten led to his downfall. He started claiming income support for ten non-existing families and incapacity benefits for ten husbands with back twinges. A suspicious benefits employee interrogated Brown's closest friends and neighbours, Cherry Blair and her husband who Brown, on an impulse, had confided in. Reluctantly they broke their promise to tell no one and betrayed him. He was found guilty of fraud and false pretences and sentenced to one month in prison, with three weeks off for good behaviour.

In the open prison he met a conman, Nick Cleggs, who taught him the tricks of his trade. Nick had fooled many with promises of a richer and better future. After his release, Brown conned his way around Britain. His main earnings area was The Kingdom of Fife, stretching from the Firth of Forth river to St Andrews up the east coast. One of his biggest and most beneficial con tricks was selling the Firth of Forth road bridge to a rich, influential American, Obama Palin. The tourist was convinced by his plausible story that the bridge was by its sell-by date and could be shipped in sections, when a vehicle tunnel was completed under the Firth of Forth.

Obama was also convinced it was a genuine deal, for he was aware that the British, for some unknown reason, were selling off their prize assets and heritage to the European Union and beyond.

The thought of going to prison for his crimes did not bother Brown, who had served a few short spells inside. The days of slopping out their body fluids were long gone. With a variety of food available, three quality meals a day, Christmas dinner and celebrations, Easter eggs, leisure facilities, EU controlled human rights to sue the taxpayer at every opportunity, he treated these interludes as stress rests. Practically anything you wanted could be smuggled in. Female visitors were greeted with open arms. With condom-filled goodies hidden in various orifices, searches were a rarity; the human rights lawyers would have rubbed their hands with glee in anticipation of another long drawn out, lucrative court case.

After being falsely accused of assault on a woman who called him a bigot and serving time, Brown's prison holidays were about to be interrupted. Pensioners living on paltry basic pensions all over Britain were about to be seen and heard in a National revolt against their shabby treatment by the Government, Social Services and the National Health Service. Pensioners in Scotland, on their starvation diet of mince and tatties, were on the move. In England, active wrinklies were wheeling frail pensioners out of hospital corridors who were suffering from neglect, malnutrition and out- of–reach thirst quenchers, to join many others on their zimmer frames and in mobility vehicles. In a combined effort they marched, drove and shuffled to prisons all over Britain, demanding permanent residence. After all they had contributed to the wealth of the country, they felt it was their human right to share the secure environment and grand lifestyle they were denied.

After many successful con tricks over a ten-year period, Jaws Brown's ego and ambition got the better of him and he planned and successfully executed the biggest con trick in history. He sold off a large quantity of Britains gold reserves at a fraction of their total value to Investment Banks in Ireland and Iceland.

From the start he was a prime suspect and under police surveillance.

With no idea that the police net was closing in on him Brown was planning to move from his native town of Kirkcaldy after selling his residence, which did not belong to him, and caused Scotland Yard great anxiety. With the recession in full swing they could no longer afford to pay junior officers more than the Prime Minister earns in overtime pay, to keep track of Brown's devious scheming, night and day.

Ken Clark, a former Chief Constable who had been demoted for his reluctance to lock up criminals and falling asleep on the job, pleaded to be allowed to do this jaw-yawning task on his basic salary, and pay his own expenses. He was desperate to atone for his past sins, including his former love affair with the Euro currency and to curry favour. His generous and unheard of offer was accepted.

Two days later Brown was in Kirkcaldy High Street, enjoying his favourite pastime, 'Now you see it. Now you don't sleight of hand tricks on the gullible public. A friend warned him that a stranger with a posh English accent and slight stammer, unkempt appearance, Hush Puppy shoes, a paunch and bags under his eyes was showing a mug-shot of Brown to the public and asking, "Have you seen this man?"

In a bit of a panic Jaws Brown rushed back to his Mansion, which he had claimed under Squatter Rights and put up for sale, unfurnished, the day before. His main priority at the moment was a quick getaway from prying eyes.

Packing his few belongings into his top of the range BMW (the bulk of his wardrobe was scattered in a number of safe houses in the Kingdom of Fife, in case of just such an emergency). In his line of work you had to be prepared for any calamity. He drove the two miles to a flat situated in Forth Avenue, in a quiet street behind the railway station, glancing anxiously in his rear mirror in case he was being followed.

George Osbourne, who lived at the flat, was a close companion who shared many of Brown's interests and hobbies. Although a very rich man who could have mixed with the jet set, Osbourne preferred to keep a low profile.

Because of his reluctance to part with his money he was shunned by his neighbours. This suited Brown, who was also aware that Osbourne knew when to keep his mouth shut.

With his BMW safely out of sight in a corner of the railway station, he spent a pleasant evening with George, discussing the dreadful state of the economy and who was responsible. Osbourne was intrigued with Jaws Brown's risk-taking lifestyle and what he had got away with. His visitor left at dawn the next morning, more than a little worried about the mysterious stranger who was stalking him. He made his way to his next refuge, on the outskirts of the town of Dunfermline, the birthplace of Andrew Carnegie, the town benefactor.

Isobella and Alex Sparring, with next door neighbour Jennie Rennie, a widow, lived in a quiet cul-de-sac. They were staunch life-long friends of Jaws Brown. He had spread much goodwill in the area by giving away large sums of money for parents to open Bank accounts for newly-born children. The Sparrings were a delightful and devoted couple who were generous to a fault. They sought no remuneration from Brown when he stayed with them. Their attitude to his lifestyle was that of Robin Hood, a legend to the people.

Jennie Rennie on the other hand got rushes of adrenaline when he let out angry outbursts of abuse against those who had let him down and betrayed his trust, on working trips south of the Scottish borders in England.

Brown sometimes stayed with her when he lay low to regain his senses after a bout of Boom or Bust excesses. Knowing his BMW would soon be traced he drove it to the town of Cowdenbeath, a few miles away. At a small back-street garage he exchanged it for cash and a clapped-out Mondeo, with no road tax or insurance, so he could blend in with the thousands of other illegal motorists and Crash for Cash insurance scammers. After a week he felt relaxed with a few drams of whisky and nightly chats on happier times, interspersed with political debate and how they could change the country for the better.

They all agreed it was no surprise that illegal immigrants were camped around the French coast as they had been doing for years, risking their necks to get into Britain. And why the bloody hell our mealy-mouthed politicians had not taken the bull by the horns years ago by stopping the influx completely. That ethnic Brits had been treated as second class citizens for decades by multi-racial obsessed governments ignoring the wishes of the electorate on most major issues. The biggest fear of them all was, as they became an ethnic minority in their own country, Middle East type chaos and bloodshed could be a future worry. As the debate got more heated the name of someone called Enoch Powell was mentioned.

A week later a dishevelled Englishman, with baggy eyes and a paunch, was seen by Jennie, acting suspiciously near the statue of Carnegie in Dunfermline Glen. The next day, wanted posters for Jaws Brown were on display all over the town. Brown was dejected; it was only a matter of time before he was spotted. Jennie, bless her, came to his rescue. She worked in a fancy dress shop and disguised him in a full-length black shroud, with only slits for his eyes. Something like a common disguise seen all over Britain, although our dithering law-makers were thinking of banning, and rightly so, hoods and masks on peaceful protest marches.

Feeling secure and invisible in his new attire. Even though it made it awkward to wear his spectacles, blow his nose or have a pee, he moved back to the east coast and another safe house in the fishing community of Largo. His English shadow was beginning to irritate him. Who was he? And what was his aim?

Connie and her sister were Essex born and bred. With their combined brood of fifteen children, all with different dads, they moved from Essex to Scotland. It was their only chance to better themselves and families. Being from a different country, England, and classed as immigrants, they were given luxury accommodation in a five star Hotel and went to the top of the housing list. Three houses were then knocked into one under the supervision of Keith Jazz, head of the council's 'Ask and get Housing Department'.

When settled in their ten-bedroom home with all mod cons, which they complained were a bit small, they sent for their parents, who were in their dotage and placed them in a free care home for the elderly. Connie's two eldest sons, Patel and Abramovich, and Shirley's teenage daughter, Kate, were soon enjoying a free education at St. Andrews University. Shirley hoped and prayed that Kate would meet a high-flying young man from a wealthy and stable background. With their subsidised council rent, income support, child benefits and payments from ten wealthy, traceable dads, through the Child Support Agency, plus the house being fully furnished by charitable organisations, the two ladies were fairly happy. A guest like Jaws Brown was always welcome. He was generous with his money, especially to the children, after all it had been tricked out of other people, so parting with it was no big deal.

Uncle Jaw, as he was known to the family, was given a warm welcome as he thrust ten-pound notes into grasping hands, with a smug smile on his face.

He was badly in need of some family comfort, after all he had been through. The children had an early tea of potato crisps, big macs with fries, twenty trays of assorted meals from Indian and Chinese takeaways, washed down by a flood of coke. They then retired to solitary confinement with their Computers and I-pods in bedrooms and playrooms all over the house. The two unmarried mothers then left their guest in a relaxed mood with a large glass of his favourite tipple, a sixty-pounds-a-bottle of vintage malt whisky.

They then went into their luxurious extended kitchen. They were about to prepare themselves for dressing the 'Essex Sandwiches', speciality of the house. The exotic ingredients were fresh and free from toxic preservatives. The secret recipe had been handed down through generations of Essex girls, making them a much sought after and talked about commodity. After a long evening of eating and drinking, a jolly threesome staggered off to bed, a giggling Shirley clutching a Computer dongle dropped by one of the kids. A few days later the identity and Ken Clark's mission became clear, in the headlines of a local newspaper, complete with his photograph and Brown's.

A few days later stalker Ken was in the news again, being asked about his relentless chase of Scotland's most notorious conman and for a conservative view on his crafty quarry. With a hasty goodbye to his hosts and their families and in a raging mood, Jaws Brown took to the road again.

Hoping to cover his tracks among golfers and tourists, he moved up to the East Coast, to Jessie Mandelson's luxury bungalow in St. Andrews. He had reluctantly bypassed the picturesque fishing villages of Crail, St. Monans, Elie, Pittenweem and Anstruther. All had taken a battering from their betrayal to the European Union's fishing fleets Armadas, by a British government. Jessie Mandelson was a divorcee from a civil marriage partner, Clair Shortcake. She was now a turncoat and Brown's part-time mistress and Banker.

He had no faith in High Street Banks who had been known to give customers bad service and get themselves into debt with client's money. Jessie supplemented her alimony by murky mortgage deals, false insurance claims and handling stolen goods. It could be said she was a lady with a corrupt sense of adventure.

After three nights of pleasure with Jessie, a tired and frustrated Brown went on a bender. He got plastered on ten pints of bitter with whisky chasers. In a drunken rage he stared at the newspaper cutting of Ken Clark and stunned Jessie with a sudden uncontrollable outburst.

"It isnae fair Jessie. That man Clark and the damned Polis are mackin' ma life a bloody misery. That Clark's got it in fur me, mac nae mistake aboot that, the man is a bloody maniac," he screamed.

With a pointed finger he jabbed Clark's photo in the throat screaming, "I hope you rot in hell, damn you!"

At that precise moment Ken Clark choked to death on a Spanish red herring outside an Anstruther fish and chip shop. When the news and timing of Clark's demise reached him the shock changed his life. He swore on his mither's life to go straight.

He bought a house in Tayport with magnificent views across the river to Dundee, and gave the rest of his money to good causes. Jaws never pointed a finger again and became known as a Tightfist. He made a living on the after-dinner circuit as a faceless speaker known only as 'the mystery man in the black shroud.'

FACT

Gordon Brown became Prime Minister of Britain after allegedly making an agreement with his predecessor Tony Blair. The democratic process of electing a new leader of the Labour Party never took place. This could have led to the destruction of the parliamentary system and the downward spiral to dictatorship.

In the recession, which took hold in 2008, Brown announced in Parliament to howls of derision from the opposition, that by lending billions of pounds of taxpayers money to Banks who had gambled with customers and shareholders money, that he had 'Saved the World financially.'

The greed and arrogant behaviour of Bankers to those they put into debt, and are indebted to, is beyond belief. In a fair and equal society they would be denied by law of continuing with their obscene bonus culture and given mental health treatment for their addictive contempt of the general public.

The New Labour Party slogan, 'Things Can Only Get Better' was one word out of tune, 'Worse' for 'Better' would have struck the right note. Apart from the billions lent to the Banks, New Labour, after an exemplary no more boom or bust start, later began spending money like there was no tomorrow, in a desperate effort to stay in power.

After his disastrous election defeat, aided by his true thoughts being broadcast accidentally to the public, Brown kept a low profile for a while. He then began lobbying to become the £270,000 a year head of the 'International Monetary Fund' to, as a spokesman was quoted, 'Stop the next financial crisis.' The Tory Party Deputy Chairman, Michael Fallon, no doubt astonished at Brown's conceit, stated,

"Mr. Brown has yet to face up to the legacy of debt he bequeathed to the taxpayers. This is a case of putting the arsonist in charge of the fire station."

The new Coalition Government brought about by disenchanted electorate of all parties was, sad to say, already up to the elbows in broken election promises they were elected on.

The British people are now seriously questioning the need for expenses-riddled Parliament, packed with men and women full of broken promises and U-turns. They have led us ever deeper into the quagmire of the European Union, with broken promises. Or that other Institution, filled with ermine-robed pensioners and known as the House of Lords, with questions asked for filling palms with silver.

Since the back-stabbing of Margaret Thatcher by her own Conservative colleagues, the British way of life has been gradually eroded away. We are now ruled, in nearly every sense of the word, by a bunch of overpaid, mindless and faceless European pen-pushers and computer converts. Why did our elected leaders not make a belated stand when we were ordered not to import bent bananas? That, with all the other senseless rules and regulations, topped by human rights being judged by them, should have awakened our politicians to their speediest U-turn ever. Did any of them feel guilty over turning their backs on the British Commonwealth? I doubt it, or making criminals out of honest British tradesmen for weighing produce in our traditional pounds and ounces. They were responsible for the death of one tradesman who died from the stress of persecution, from their cowardly acceptance of all things European Union.

One of my greatest delights in life is to listen to imported American television programmes. The greatest and largest English speaking country in the World still speaks and acts non-metric. The Americans have a greater respect for our heritage and way of life than our elected rabble, who have discarded our British rights to the dustbin.

The American attitude should make those who betrayed the British way of life, which was fought and sacrificed for through two World Wars, hang their heads in shame.

Expense scandals at the heart of power, of bribery and corruption questions asked of forces of the law. Hacking phones by newspapers to the darkest depths, all three in connection left the public in distress.

Referendums promised, then arrogantly refused by oily tongues that slickly turn in upon themselves.

If only they had listened to the voters point of view, who sensed what was coming long before we knew, we would not all now be drowning in a bureaucratic Euro stew.

THE DIAMOND COMPANY

FRED There is something strange going on across the road Doris.

DORIS For goodness sake Fred, stop being nosy and get me a cup of tea.

FRED A gang of men have barricaded themselves in on the pavement and dug all the slabs up.

DORIS So what! Who is it this time, gas, water or electric?

FRED You might as well get up and see for yourself, it's pension day, time to spend, spend and spend.

DORIS Ha! Ha! Ha! Very funny, I'm not budging till I've had my cup of tea.

FRED There's a young yob dragging a fully-grown Rottweiler along the gutter. I think it's reluctant to meet it's next victim.

DORIS Maybe he's training it to be a guide dog.

FRED One of the gang has started up a little machine and it's scooping a trench down the middle of the pavement.

DORIS Well, you never know, they might be scooping a doggie trench and if they are still there tomorrow they might come across your remains if you don't put the damned kettle on. Who the hell are they?

FRED Well it's not the usual lot, or the council, but there is a big sign saying they're digging for diamonds.

DORIS Come off it Fred, don't make me laugh. There is as much chance of finding diamonds under those slabs as us getting a decent pension.

FRED No need to be sarcastic, I'm just telling you what it says.

DORIS Sarcastic, who's sarcastic? Just imagine all the doggie trots under slab level. What does it say on those scoop bins? Clean up after your dog. Crap a slab more like.

FRED Come on Doris, you know you are a dog lover at heart.

DORIS I am! I am! I have always gone out of my way for under dogs and I don't believe that they should be trodden on.

FRED I bet there is nothing you would like to see more than them all pampered to death.

DORIS You're right there, now stop nattering and get me a cuppa.

FRED Edwina Curry has just come out of Major's at No 10, what with the barricades and all, she doesn't know if she's coming or going.

DORIS Well it gets harder to make up your mind as you get older, but credit where it's due, she has been a good neighbour to John over the years, they are always in and out of each others. She also helps feed those fat cats of his, I don't know where he finds the money to keep them all.

FRED Oh no, not him again.

DORIS Not who again?

FRED That young trouble maker Tony Blair's just turned up. He is giving poor old John a right ear bashing. Hang on a minute, I don't believe it, I think he is actually trying to help John find a way out of No 10.

DORIS Trying to get him buried more like. Ten years hard labour would wipe that permanent grin off his face.

FRED That Gillian Shepherd's just come out from behind her net curtains. She is giving the workmen a right tongue lashing. Just as well she lost her walking stick when some kids mugged her last week.

DORIS Fred, that's not funny, that could have been me.

FRED Well, kids will be kids, probably it's just the modern way of playing tag. It's a hard life for kids nowadays, what with all the temptations they face and rich food that we never had. It's even driving the ruddy cows mad.

DORIS Got an answer for everything haven't you Fred, you will be telling me next that it's a good job we have plenty of do gooders, to mollycoddle the little blighters.

FRED Ken's just come out of No 11, showing some interest, he is looking a bit flushed, bet he has been on the booze filling that big belly again before the prices go up in tomorrow's budget. Isn't he supposed to be on a budget diet?

DORIS I believe he is, according to Tessa May who just opened that new shoe shop.

FRED He looks a bit top heavy to me. It's hard to believe he once ran a national health club. I think I will have a word with him and try to find out what the heck's going on.

DORIS For goodness sake shut the window, you're letting all the hot air out and you're not going anywhere until I get my morning cup of tea in bed, then you can set about the tripe and onions ready for lunch.

FRED Here you are Doris, sorry there's no milk, the milkman's late, bet he's digging for diamonds. I'll be back in a jiffy.

DORIS Anymore cracks like that and you'll be digging in the airing cupboard for sheets and blankets for the spare bed.

FRED I'm back Doris, are you up yet?

DORIS No, I'm not, Have you found out yet what is happening?

FRED Well, I've heard some tall stories in my time but this lot takes the biscuit. The workers said straight-faced that that they are really digging for underground television, best I've heard since Rupert Murdock sent his son to buy him a sky line. Ken got excited again and began to stammer a load of nonsense.

DORIS Cheeky devils. What's all this about a sky
line?

FRED Well, Rupert sent his son to the corner shop
for a sky line. His son asked him what it was
for. Murdock told him 'tongue in cheek' it
was for capturing sky. His son fell for it hook,
line and sinker.

DORIS Well we all know with Rupert the sky's the
limit.

FRED There is something fishy going on. I can't put
my finger on it but there is not a bum cleavage
in sight and not one of these men are leaning
on a shovel. I'm going to the Police Station, it
might be open by now.

DORIS Alright, but mind what you are stepping into
and bring back some milk, I'll have another
cuppa before I get up.

FRED GAMBLES
2008

Samantha Silk, or 'Hot Totty' as she was known to her male colleagues, pulled the collar of her coat up to her chin in a vain attempt to keep herself warm. It was a beautiful night, but there was a definite chill in the air. She shook her head slightly and a lock of blonde curls fell across her face, blocking her vision. Pushing her tresses impatiently out of her eyes, she sighed softly and looked up at the sky. Samantha had never seen anything that looked more awesome. There was a full moon shimmering silently above her and a smattering of stars sparkling like diamonds displayed on a cloak of black velvet. She was so caught up in her appreciation of its beauty, she almost didn't catch the subtle rustling in the bushes to her far left. With churning stomach and cold perspiration trickling down her face, she slowly turned to view the bushes and walked hesitantly towards them.

As a young, desk-bound policewoman, her blonde hair and slim but curvy figure had thrust her into this plain-clothes duty as bait for a serial molester. The fiend had been creating terror in the suburbs of the city for over a year. The only clue to the molester was notes stuck in the victim's backs, with the words in capitals, FRED THE SHRED, in red ink. The victims were attacked at random, from Samantha look-alike to pensioners, children with bank accounts and a young man with bleached hair and a feminine walk.

Samantha Silk was following a family tradition by joining the Force.

Her grandfather had been a Force legend in his time. An old-fashioned beat bobby, he had controlled his patch by knowing all the locals by name and their varied religions.

After a few clips around the ears and on rare occasions a kick up the rear, from an early age the youths on his beat respected him and his uniform. The co-operation of parents who in those days were all ardent supporters of 'Spare the rod, spoils the child' had made his job much respected and pleasant to dispatch.

As Samantha approached the bushes the smell of hot curry swept over her and her heart skipped a beat. Suddenly, a fox darted from the undergrowth across her feet with the leftovers of an Indian takeaway clamped in its jaws. Shaking from shock, she hoped that her back-up of one part-time policeman was near at hand for quick assistance if needed. Her feet were already aching from the high-heeled shoes she had been asked to wear by her superiors, as these appeared to be another of the molester's fetishes.

As she continued her lonely walk she thought of her ambition to be a member of the 'Family Car Control Force', the S.A.S. of the uniformed branch. A successful capture of the molester would speed her to this goal and a career in a comfortable police car. Because of suspicion in the Force that the molester somehow seemed aware, on previous attempts to catch him, or possibly her, of police movements, Samantha was not allowed radio contact with her back-up. This made her feel very vulnerable. She was grateful that the moonlight gave her some protection. Except for city centre headquarters, all police stations in a ten-mile radius were closed due to lack of funding. 'The thin blue line' of police, like a protected species, was rarely seen.

Thousands of people would turn up at sporting events hoping to catch a glimpse of them, and many children grew up believing that all police were legless, because they only saw the top half of their bodies as they passed by in Panda cars. At that very moment, thousands of Panda cars and their crews all over the country were discreetly hidden near main roads. Their main priority, to keep a bleary eye open for 'Speed Camera Fanatics'. This growing band of tormented people were now a threat to government funding. Thousands of Speed Cameras were being stolen or destroyed on the spot.

As Samantha reached the first of the densely-populated 'Road Hump' streets, now eerily quiet, she became very tense. No-one in their right mind now walked the pavements of 'Road Hump' streets after dark.

This had come about after protesters started digging up the suspension-ruining, exhaust spewing of fumes and jolting of disabled passengers caused by council 'Road Humps'. The local council, at great expense, quickly replaced them. After a while the protesters had realised they were making a grave error of judgement. As the road humps were so close together, they decided it would be easier to tarmac in between them, creating a level surface once again. The council in their wisdom rebuilt the 'Humps' on top. With both sides unwilling to give in, the streets were now four feet higher than the pavements. The shadowed pavements now hid a multitude of general low-life, human and pests. Tarmac became a scarce commodity, travelling families unable to buy their main source of income, turned to crime. Some of them in desperation raided isolated farmhouses to trap roosting House Martins and Pigeons to devour, also stealing anything they could find, at the risk of being unlawfully shot.

Suddenly Samantha saw in the distance the head and shoulders of a lone figure, the shoulders hunched against the cold night air. As the figure drew nearer, a shiver of fear ran down her spine. It appeared to be wearing what looked like a loose-fitting, ankle length black dress. In contrast the head shone like a beacon in the moonlight, making it impossible to distinguish any features. At that moment Samantha was glad she had kept on her regulation police underwear, complete with suspenders. Tucked securely in her right suspender was the comforting feeling of her 'Panda Protective Stiletto'. She was as pure as the driven snow and many of her future Panda car male partners would swear to the Stiletto's sharpness.

Samantha relaxed and smiled as the 'sinister'-looking figure approached her. It was the parish priest in his flowing cassock, his bald head shining and his best-selling book in hand.

He was returning from the Swallow pub, in the nearby village of Thurnby, after a late-night sermon there, on the evils of drink. After a short chat he went on his way, swaying unsteadily from side to side.

As she left the 'Road Hump' streets off the Portway Road it was a relief to walk on a level pavement again. She made her way to what was once a busy police station, but was now a council rent arrears office. At the back of the building a hut was still used by Panda car patrols for a well-earned cuppa and to relax until their shift was over.

Samantha was looking forward to making herself a nice strong cup of tea. Waiting in the shadows of the empty hut was an agitated figure wearing face make-up and a blonde wig.

Fred Gamble had served the community for many years as a loyal and trusted Bank Manager, looking after customers' deposit and mortgage loans as if they were his own. He appreciated his well-paid job and the esteem in which his clients held him. To give something back to society he became a volunteer Special Constable in the Police

Force in his spare time. There was a dramatic change in his personality during the credit crunch in 2008, when his failing bank was merged with another and he lost his job. The shock of this, and his pent-up anger at his Bank superiors awarding themselves huge sums of money for losing shareholders hard-earned money, caused him to have a nervous breakdown.

During this time his wife of many years became puzzled as to why her tights and undies became stretched and baggy for no apparent reason. She had been using the same British brand most of her adult life with no problems. It all became clear when she caught her startled husband cross-dressing in her underwear. Betty Gamble found it very hard to deal with her husband's mood swings and disruptive behaviour since he lost his job, and this discovery was too much for her to take. Shaking her bleached-blonde head in disbelief she told Fred to leave the family home.

Alone in a dingy bedsit Fred Gamble's other self became an obsession. The daring and dangerous Transvestite as he called her, gradually became the dominant side of the staid ex-Bank Manager's character. Fred Gamble knew from his police contacts of Samantha Silk's route that night.

He had taken the precaution of sending an urgent message by radio to Samantha's back-up, PC Ian Blair, supposedly from Police Headquarters, sending him on a wild goose chase to apprehend two burly men acting suspiciously in an unmarked car.

The first Samantha knew of her attacker's presence was an arm tightly encircling her neck from behind, dragging her deeper into the shadows. Her molester was muttering dire threats if she dared to resist. As he pawed at her breasts with his free hand, the smell of Chanel perfume and garlic breath against her cheek made her senses reel. With the ever-tightening arm across her throat, she felt herself slipping into a dark, bottomless pit. She wriggled frantically to reach up her skirt and managed to grasp her Panda Protective Stiletto. With a twisting motion she stabbed backward into her molester's groin. With her legs like jelly she gasped for breath as Gamble released his stranglehold and collapsed, screaming in agony, half castrated.

Samantha kicked off her shoes and stumbled towards a 'Road Hump' street, seeking help. From a vantage point on top of a 'Hump' she saw a convoy of lights in the distance. Fifty Panda cars were heading towards her as they returned from 'Speed Camera' patrol. She sank to her knees from shock and relief, the bloody Stiletto still clutched in her hand.

A few years later, after a series of free operations on the National Health service, a Transvestite Gamble was front-page news in the National newspapers as she partied happily with a host of Britain's most notorious criminals in Broadmoor Mental Prison.

By coincidence, at the same time a newly-promoted Police Sergeant Samantha Silk was on full-pay compassionate leave from the 'Family Car

Control Force'. While her five million pounds claim for racial discrimination and prejudice against the Muslim Chief of Police, for being passed over for quicker promotion, and his attitude towards her free-flowing blonde hair, was settled.

PROLOGUE

The following tale is a part of one of my stories in the book and E-book titled the 'THE DREAM MAKER'. The contents are in harmony with the theme of this book.

It is based on an immigrant family of near-on two decades, whom I befriended. The names of the family have been changed for their privacy and are now characterised. This also gave me the opportunity to write on a number of annoying and topical subjects in a humorous manner.

Dad Genta, Mum Bargan, the fourteen years old son Willnot and his three sisters Dunsay, nine, Gabby, five and Seetoo three have just had their lives turned upside down. Due to cheap Chinese imports, Genta's once lucrative Hosiery business has gone bankrupt. They have lost everything, including a gated mansion, their top-of-the-range limousine and pet pony.

DOWN IN THE DUMPS

The children were not happy with their new lifestyle. After being used to having everything they wanted, it was hard to go without. Willnot and Dunsay felt lost with no mobile phones. Gabby was getting on everyones nerves with her endless questions and asking why when she got an answer.

Three years old Seetoo was into pulling Dunsay's and Gabby's hair, kicking shins and crying for hours on end if she did not get her own way.

Dad Genta did not see much of his family as he worked day and night to get the family back on their feet. When they did see him, he was a big softie and let them do as they pleased.

Mum Bargan was having a hard time trying to keep the peace. It was testing her patience to the limit. She did not seem to have a minute to herself. The children could not get used to the hustle and bustle of the large multi-racial school after the small village one where everybody knew each other. The majority of pupils were of Indian origin, with quite a number of Caribbean and African children whose great-grandparents migrated to Britain in the 1950s and 1960s.

A handful of white children could also be seen and a surprising number of mixed race. This said a lot about social harmony in the area. The children missed their friends from the village school, Willnot most of all. From being the most popular boy at school, he was now just another face amongst hundreds. He had also attracted the attention of the school bullies who thought he was too clever for his own good.

Dunsay was also in trouble. A report from the new school told her parents just how far behind the rest of her age group she had become in her studies.

THE ITSY BITSY MAN

As he walked the short distance for his meeting with Dunsay, Robbie Martin wondered what he had let himself in for. He was a pretty fit old man who, the day before, had cycled the twenty-odd miles around Rutland Water, with it's fishing, sailing and bird-watching stops. The last time he had ridden a bike, they only had three gears. The one he had hired had ten, which were difficult for him to master. As he felt a little saddle-sore and leg weary, he was not in the best of moods. A widower, he lived happily on his own, enjoying his many hobbies and exciting over-fifties holidays. Amongst other things, he had written a children's book called 'The Itsy Bitsy Family. Feeling rather pleased with himself, he had some printed which he gave away to the families of local children. He became known as 'The Itsy Bitsy Man'.

Dansay's mum, having seen one of the books and a later one called 'The Roof Tops' when the family moved into the area, asked him if he would help Dansay with her homework. After much thought, he agreed to help, telling Bargan not to expect to see any great improvement.

He was not a teacher, having spent most of his life working in a factory. He rang the doorbell feeling really nervous.

As he walked into the dining room, Dunsay's first thought was, "blimey, he must be about ninety years old." He was short and stocky with thinning grey hair and faded blue eyes. She dreaded to think what questions Gabby would ask him when she got the chance.

Robbie got to know the family well, teaching Dunsay four nights a week after school. He taught her by asking her to repeat the alphabet and her spelling over and over again until she knew them without thinking. Although she wanted to be clever and not have her classmates sniggering about her for being stupid, Dunsay did not like spending so much time on her homework. After school, she just wanted to play, watch the television and relax.

Robbie was also wise to all her tricks to cheat and copy to get by. He was born in Scotland where he lived until, aged twelve, the family moved to England as there was no work for his three teenage sisters. Although he had lived in Leicestershire most of his life, he kept his Scottish accent and sayings. When he got angry with her, he would start speaking in his native tongue. "Noo look here, lassie, if ye think am cummin here tae waste ma time, ye've got anither think cummin". He would also greet them by saying, "Hello, the noo".

At Gabby's birthday party, they found he could be fun, joining in the games and singing silly songs like "fur ye canna shuv yer grannie aff a bus", and the Kelty Clippie, which was about the old days in Scotland when they had ladies who were paid to ride on the buses, ring the bell to let you on and off, and give you a ticket from a little machine strapped to them and clip it. They also had to put up with a lot of jokes and ribbing from the tough coal-dust covered miners who used the buses before they were provided with the luxury of pit baths.

GABBY HAS HER SAY

After a week, Gabby and Seetoo started to sit at the table as Robbie taught Dunsay. Seetoo sat in silence, staring at Robbie as if he was from outer space. After a few nights, she placed a book in front of Robbie before sitting down. Robbie got the message and started to teach her as well. She became an eager and clever pupil. Gabby, on the other hand, thought she knew it all, trying to tell Robbie what to do. The moment Dunsay had been dreading arrived. Gabby started asking personal questions, "Robbie, why is your hair growing out of your nose and ears but not on top of your head?" Dunsay gave a sigh of relief when he smiled and said, "when you get to my age Gabby, everything starts growing downwards and starts to sag, it is something you can look forward to".

"Do you keep your teeth in a glass by the side of your bed or in the bathroom?" "No", he replied, "and the tooth fairy is not getting them yet, you can try and take them but they might bite your fingers off".

"But why have you still got your own teeth at your age?" "Because I don't eat all the sweet sickly food that you do".

"Why are you blind?"

"I'm not blind", said a puzzled Robbie.

"Why do you put your glasses on to read with? You must be blind".

"How do you manage to put your shoes and socks on?"

"Who does your washing and ironing?"

"Who tells you to get up in the mornings if you live on your own?"

"Why do you live on your own, does nobody love you?"

Gabby was in full flow. Dunsay nudged Gabby with her elbow, telling her out of the side of her mouth to shut up, but she took no notice.

"Why do you come here when we want to play?"

Before an angry-looking Robbie could answer, Dunsay shouted for mum to take Gabby away. That night she told Gabby to think about what she was going to say before opening her big mouth and upsetting people. As she drifted into a restless sleep, Dunsay was visited by the Dream Maker and taken to a place full of strange creatures

THE JABBERING GABBIES

She found herself standing in front of a large sign
at the entrance of a long street of expensive houses.
The sign said in huge letters:
THE STREET OF ALL TALK.

CAPITAL OF GABBY LAND

You're in the land of Gabbies
Beware of what we ask
When answering our questions
But why we will throw back.
We are three feet tall
With eyes on stalks
And mouths the size of buckets
Our teeth are covered in sugar
As they rock in their sockets.
We like turkey twizzlers
Fried chips by the ton
Don't like veg or gravy
Or a man called Jamie
When we see him, we just run.
Please enjoy your visit
We hope you have some fun
But you won't get a word in edgeways
As our mouths go on the run.

Dunsay walked slowly down the street. On the other side, a stream of strange-looking creatures carrying sheets of blank paper were going into a house jabbering non-stop. They took no notice of her and seemed full of their own importance.

When she was nearly opposite house No.10, a crowd of Jabbering Gabbies gathered around her from the other houses, barring her way. With their beady eyes glowing red from all night jabbering sessions, sticking out ears, sharp pointed fingers and bucket sized mouths, they were a terrifying sight. They all shouted at her as one voice :

"How did you get here?"
"Are you on your own?"
"Where's your mum and dad?"
"Have you a return ticket?"
"Are you legal?"
"Where is your passport?"
"Do you have an identity card?"
"Do you want some money or a cream cake and
fizzy drink?"
"Have you signed on?"
"Have you been to Social Services?"
"Do you know your human rights?"

She could not escape as the questioning went on and on. With their rotten teeth wobbling in their festering gums, Gabbies were breathing out a foul smell and lots of hot air. The smell became so bad she felt faint. After what seemed like a lifetime, the Gabbies all shouted, "Why? Why? Why?" , then let her make her way to the street entrance. Dunsay woke up in a cold sweat and looked across the bedroom. She was more than pleased to see Gabby sleeping peacefully, looking her normal self.

PLANET TWO FACED

As Dunsay fell asleep one night, feeling sorry for Willnot and his pimply face, she heard the whispering voice of the Dream Maker.

"Dunsay, you are going on a long journey. Do not worry about your brother, his face will soon clear up. It is just nature's way to let us know we are not perfect and nobody can tell what fate has in store for them. Teenagers sometimes get too full of themselves and need bringing back to reality with a zit or two. You are going to a planet on the other side of the universe. On it live tribes of ugly creatures. They are power mad, greedy, destructive and vain. Weapons of mass destruction are made and stockpiled which could destroy themselves and the planet they live on. It is by a freak of nature it exists. With all it's past savagery, it is a miracle that it has survived this long. You will be flying there in a Blue Bottle spacecraft."

"Will I be able to see you this time?"

"No, child, I have no shape or form as you know it. Through centuries in time I moved into an advanced life form. My voice is real but my identity must be left to your imagination. What you see is

112

what you get. I will try to protect you from the many dangers that await on your adventure."

These comforting words made Dunsay feel at ease as she entered the cabin of the spacecraft at the bottom of the garden, the powerful wings flapping, ready for take-off. She was surprised to find there were other passengers aboard and a stewardess. When she first set eyes on the stewardess and the other passengers, it made her wonder if the Dream Maker was trying to get her used to the strange creatures she was told she would see on Planet Two Faced.

Silla Blackfly welcomed her aboard and introduced her to a party of Beatles. Silla, with her ball-like cheeks, buck teeth and big smile was not like a usual stewardess. Her high-pitched voice rose to a shriek sometimes but was warm and friendly.

"If there is anything you need on the journey, luvvie, just push the red button on your fully reclining seat," she said with a smile as she introduced her to the Beatles.

They were a friendly bunch and once she got used to their creepy crawly looks, Dunsay was able to relax. The for of them were smartly dressed in short black jackets with drainpipe trousers, white shirts and winkle-picker shoes. Thick mops of hair framed their faces.

They were being dropped off in India where they hoped to find peace of mind through the teachings of a holy man who lived in a cavern in silent meditation.

His name was Jappa Nogo and his only possessions

were a begging bowl and a brand new Rolls Royce given to him by a grateful worshipper. Like Silla, they all spoke a language called Pudlian which was a sing-song type of English and difficult to understand.

"I am taking them to the bar and eating lounge upstairs", shrieked Silla, "by the time they have had a drink and are liver full, it will be time to drop them off."

Later, Dunsay heard them shouting at the top of their voices, "We all live in a yellow submarine", over and over again. She shook her head sadly, thinking if that were true, no wonder they were going so far to seek help.

The Beatles were in ecstasy when they reached India, thinking they would be in strawberry fields with blue skies after Jappa Nogo had set their minds at rest.

As they settled down in the spacecraft for the long trip through space, Silla told Dunsay that the Beatles only knew the holy man through a chance meeting with a long-forgotten friend called Adam the Ant who had visited the cavern and was so enlightened he more or less vanished from the face of the earth. They were hoping their blind date would give them as big a buzz.

When the Blue Bottle landed on Planet Two Faced, Silla Blackfly shrieked goodbye in her sing-song voice to a slightly anxious Dunsay from the Blue Bottle before it flew off into a purple-coloured sky.

A frightened Dunsay found herself standing on the planet's smooth, plastic-like surface. There was nothing but a bare wilderness all round. As she stood shivering with fear, a small black dot appeared on the horizon, getting bigger by the minute. When it got near enough to make out what it was, she screamed from fright. It was a multi-coloured bug with ten legs, four arms, strapped to a carriage in a harness. The jogging bug skidded to a halt, looked her over, then snapped at her, "Well get in , what are you waiting for? I haven't got all day."

"What are you and why are you here?", asked a cringing Dunsay.

"Huh, didn't that dozy Dream Maker tell you? I'm Septic Sam, your tour guide. Whatever you do, don't think about touching me, let alone cuddle, it would mean the end for you."

With its ten wriggly legs, feet with four square toes, twenty-fingered hands, squinty eyes, flat nose and sharp pointed teeth, Sam was the most ugly, repulsive thing anyone could imagine.

Dunsay was now feeling more angry than scared at the ill-mannered way this ugly bug was speaking to her.

"You should be so lucky, the thought of touching you makes me feel sick."

"Huh", he replied, "you should take a good look at yourself, you humans were all born in a brainstorm. You're also short on arms, legs and hands, and must have been at the back of the queue when good looks were handed out. To tell you the truth, you lot are every bugs nightmare."

"Well, if that's what you think, why did you take on the job of driving me around this horrible place?"

"Because", snarled Sam, "the way things are going this planet is heading for its last orbit around the eyeballs. It's drying up here in the South and there is a food shortage. I'm ruddy well starving. Not that you have to worry, if I ate you, it would make me a lot sicker than I already am. Your Dream Maker has promised me free transport to your place. I'm not looking forward to it, but a starving bug can't be choosy. Besides, from what I've been told, there is plenty of bacteria to eat there, as you humans are not mean with your waste and rubbish, and enjoy dropping it willy-nilly all over your streets and planet."

Dunsay decided to keep quiet. She could not argue with what he just said. They were moving along at a steady pace with Septic Sam's legs going ten to the dozen.

After a while, she tried to cheer up the miserable bug by being pleasant to him.

"I must say your roads are lovely and smooth. I can hardly tell we are moving. Our roads are full of potholes. Some feeble old people go to prison because they refuse to pay to help patch them up. What are these lovely roads made of?"

This made him grumpier than ever.

"Well, if you must know, they are made from chopped down whiskers, bristle, fluff, dry skin and plucked eyebrow waste. This is used as layers of hard-core before the top surface is laid on top. The hard smooth surface that you think is so lovely and is playing hell with my feet is just a crying waste of this planet's resources and the reason I'm starving. It's a mixture of cut skin, layers of fat from the double chin, jowls and eyebags, plus lots of bone hacked from Big Nose mountain. It is boiled in steaming sweat bubbles, then mixed with shingles from the East and West coast. While it is still steaming, foreign labourers from Dire land called Tarmaccadams lay it and roll it flat."

"Well, thanks for being so kind and telling me", said Dunsay as she glared at the back of Sam's head as he trotted along. "Where is your home?", she asked politely.

"I lived at a Hos-Spit-Hall until I became septic."

"Are you taking me there now?"

"You must be joking", he snorted. "Why do you think I'm septic? Do you think I like being an untouchable?"

What's that got to do with me? It's not my fault you are such an ugly septic bug."

Septic Sam screeched to a halt, his feet skidding all over the road.

"Oh, so you think it's not your fault do you?" He turned to face her, sparks flying off his teeth as his outrage got the better of him.

"I've met your type before, hundreds of times. We let you into our Hos-Spit-Halls free of charge, feed you and nurse you back to health. We even allow visits so you won't get lonely. What do we get in return? You walk in from your germ-ridden houses and your dirty chewing-gum trodden streets, or moaning and crying on trolleys to beat us up in a drunken fury as we try to help you, then you sit, lie and tread on us as if we were muck. That's how I got septic and was thrown out of my Hos-Spit-Hall."

By this time Sam was foaming at the mouth because of the sheer injustice of it all.

"You don't even have the common sense to wash your hands, let alone have a good scrub down before you arrive. The Dream Maker also promised to search heaven and earth to find me an antiseptic Hos-Spit-Hall where I can be treated and become my old self again and live there for the rest of my life. After all, I was born to live off bacteria, not die from it."

Dunsay was about to give a nasty reply, but thought better of it. He was mad enough as it was.

They moved along in silence for about an hour before she plucked up the courage to ask him. "Well, where are we going then?"

Septic Sam had calmed down and answered in a more pleasant voice.

"As you landed in the county of East Earlobe, we travelled south for a while and are now heading West to Cheeky Land. There we will meet the Boil tribes of Plooks, Zits and Pimples. You will see the reason we are all starving on the way. All the dense forests of Beards, Bristles and Baby Fluff are being hacked down at an alarming rate to make the new roads that you think are so lovely. The nooks, crannies, lines and wrinkles are being smoothed away, and old bits and bobs swept up behind the Earlobe Counties to the East and West of the planet. Everywhere our bacteria food supply grows is being destroyed. Our only chance of survival is to flee to another planet, or invade the North of this one, which has an unending, high-protein food supply, but is a dangerous place to live, with fearsome warrior tribes. Other Worlds don't want us, they say we are vermin and pests, just out to take advantage of the inhabitants and live off them. It looks like there is no choice but a civil war between the united tribes in the South and the Nits and Lice highlanders in the North.

The united tribes were ready to invade the Hairy Highlands to try and defeat the Nits and Lice. They had to move quickly, the South was becoming so smooth and tightly packed, they were finding it difficult to get a grip with their jelly-like underbellies.

As they entered Cheeky Land, Dunsay saw a large shape shimmering in the light of three small suns in the purple sky. Before she could ask, Septic Sam told her it was Big Nose mountain with two huge gaping tunnels of Nostril underneath.

"I will take you there later", he said.

They looked down on Dimple City, which seemed to be made up of a maze of street corners. They saw gangs of Hoods around, looking like black shadows.

"I think we will carry on ", said Sam. "It's just as well we don't have identity cards yet, they would be no good to them, they all look the same."

He headed North, rounding the swollen, massive , glistening red lips of Lipland and the wide gob of Garbage Canyon in the middle.

"It was too dangerous," he remarked, "to go any nearer this area. There might be a Garbage throwback or a sudden attack by the Dreaded Cold Sores at any time."

As they moved on towards the Tunnels of Nostrils and Big Nose mountain, Dunsay sat back in the carriage and relaxed as Septic Sam worked up a lather as he galloped along. She was beginning to like the grumpy old bug and his sharp way of speaking to her.

"You're not as bad as you're painted", she told him.

"For an ugly human, you're not so bad yourself", he replied.

This was the biggest compliment she would get out of him and she knew it, but it was better than nothing.

She trusted him now and he seemed very concerned about both their safety. Tired out, she dozed off until they jolted to a stop. When she opened her eyes, she found herself staring into the great entrance to one of the Tunnels of Nostril. It was an incredible sight. The walls and floor were covered in a hairy fungus.

There was a strong current of air which tried to pull them into the Tunnel one minute then blow them away the next.

Septic Sam told her that it was thought the Tunnels stretched all the way to the top of Big Nose mountain. Nobody had ever been brave enough to get inside to find out. They were thought to be haunted. Late at night, and sometimes during the day, a noise like thunder could be heard roaring down the Tunnels, like the wailing of a giant dinosaur mortally wounded. This went on for hours on end, even right through the night.

The Tunnels also gave out Sneezers.

"The muffled and the blaster", said Sam. "A full blaster can give you a virus from thirty feet away.

Many strange skeleton parts were often discovered at the entrances.

"Let's get away from here, quick", said Dunsay, "you're making me feel sick."

For the first time, she thought she heard Sam chuckling as they walked away. Could he be laughing at her and making it all up to annoy her?

She was surprised how much he knew. Maybe that was why the Dream Maker got him to show her around and was going to so much trouble for him.

Sam gave her a fixed stare before they set off.

"The Dream Maker is not going to be very happy if I don't take you on the full tour. The trouble is, I can't be sure of your safety in these troubled times and she will be less happy with me if you come to any harm, but it's up to you if we carry on."

"We might as well finish what we started", said Dunsay. She was very keen on visiting the hairy highlands after what Sam told her on the way to Chinland.

They travelled along a well-worn track that ran along the left hand side of Big Nose mountain up to the state of Eye Balls. At the moment, the whites around the sea blue interiors were tinged with red from lack of sleep. The lids kept blinking rapidly in a nervous manner. The worry of the coming war had upset the balance of the all-seeing eyes. They would have to watch the horror of all-out war. There was one blessing however, the tears of sorrow would wash away most of the deadly chemicals that poured down from the battlefield from the Forehead Trenches.

Alas, Sam, Dunsay and carriage were sighted as they left the sparse cover of the Plucked Eyebrows and captured by a Hairy Highland patrol.

After many adventures good and bad, when Dunsay escaped being scalped by a hairbreadth, thanks to Septic Sam they broke free from the clutches of King Nitwit and his Queen Salad Dodger and made their way back to Big Nose mountain. The Dream Maker had promised to have them rescued in three days time, from a high flat-topped cutaway ridge, by the Blue Bottle spacecraft.

Two days later, from their vantage point, they witnessed the battle of the North-South divide.

THE HAIRY HIGHLANDS

This country had the most colourful scenery on the planet. All the hairy trees, tufts, wisps and strands were a mixture of wonderful colours. Some were interwoven in braids, others hung loose and shiny, a few held back in tight bunches. Forests of dreadlocks.

It was also, apart from the few fierce tribes who lived there, the most dangerous landscape on the planet. Ruled with a firm bite by King Nitwit.

His grandfather, a Hairy Highlands curling champion, seized power in the 1960s from Scargill the Thatch, king of the underground. Grandad Teasy Weasy, with the help of self-made chemicals, soon had the whole nation under his spell by perfumed smells and colours invented in his hairdressing salon.

When King Nitwit came to power after the poisoning of his father, King Bald Spot, he experimented with his grandad's chemicals until they became more dangerous than ever. He was now armed with the biggest stockpile of chemical warfare in the universe.

You name it, King Nitwit made it; dyes of all the colours of the rainbow and many never seen before.

Bleach, Blonde, Black, White, Brunette, Red, Purple, Green and the lethal Blue Rinse. Global warming sprays, Brylsheen and enough shampoo from Dry, Wet, Soft, Hard, Thickening, Medicated, to smother the whole planet ten times over.

Unfortunately, spillages over many years from underground pipelines had seeped into the scalp, making the once heather-covered highland a poisoned wonderland. Travelling in this many-coloured jungle could get you into a lot of trouble. Even the Nits and Lice tread carefully through it, making detours to get around the troublesome Bleach Blonde thickets which could trap and devour them. But surviving and adapting to this chemical cocktail was a never-ending supply of the most vitamin nourishing food on the planet. It was so good, the Northern tribes only allowed their young small amounts or they would have become obese overnight.

King Teasy Weasy was the man responsible for doubling its quantity during his reign.

The King and his generals decided that the battle must be fought from the Trenches of Forehead before the Boils and their offshoots could cross the scalp line into the dense undergrowth of the Hairy Highlands. The seasoned warriors of the Blue Rinse Brigade, backed up by the Nicola Sturgeon royal guard would lead the attack in a spearhead formation. They would charge into the middle of the enemy and try to break through their ranks.

He made his generals sign a pledge that, if

anything happened to him in the battle, his huge stockpile of weapons of mass destruction would be washed out and destroyed. The risk of them falling into the hands of some suicidal mad tribe were too great, they could destroy the whole planet.

An army of Nit Nurses, looking spotlessly clean in their starched white uniforms, stand in lines behind their warriors. Commander Ann the Wink was a strict taskmaster. With her beady little eyes enlarged by magnifying glasses, she commanded through fear. Only a few Nits passed the tough training courses. Even their homes were inspected before being picked. Ann the Wink recruited only the best. They had to be dedicated as the job was dangerous with little reward. She did not allow any weak links in her team, sending them packing with a few harsh words and a curt nod of her head. Carrying Burberry handbags filled with superglue to stick the wounded together, the Nit Nurses would bravely put their lives at risk above and beyond the call of duty as they trotted onto the battlefield, dragging the patched-up wounded to safety. The only weapon they used was their headbutt, known as the Glasgow Kiss. Ann the Wink worked with the hardest-headed Nits in the land. If she survived, this would be her last battle. Well by her sell-by date, she was looking forward to retirement at a charity run BBC, a Bed and Breakfast Colony on Benefits Island off the coast of Mugsland.

The battle had cost both sides dearly, losing a lot of their bravest. Ann the Wink and Simon the

Plook died linked together as she headbutted him into submission and he smothered her with his zipper-like mouth. The battlefield was littered with Nit Nurses and Burberry bags and their scattered contents of superglue.

Dunsay and Septic Sam watched the battle in silent dismay all day long. If only King Nitwit had offered to help his neighbour earlier and got rid of his weapons under the watchful eyes of all involved, it would never have happened. The full horror of what they saw would live with them forever. Septic Sam was right about fighting; in the end, nobody wins, but everybody loses.

When the Blue Bottle spacecraft came into sight, a relieved Dunsay could not wait to climb aboard and head for home. Silla Blackfly welcomed them aboard, asking Dunsay if she had enjoyed the dream trip, at the same time making sure that Septic Sam didn't come within touching distance.

"Yes, thank you, but I'm really glad to see you again", thinking how could you explain to anybody what she had seen and been through.

Silla told them they would be picking the party of Beatles up on the journey back before taking Dunsay home. She had also had great news for Septic Sam from the Dream Maker.

After travelling the length and breadth of the land, she found an Anti Septic Hos-Spit-Hall. It stood near a Blue Flag beach called Clearwater. Next to it was a large estate of new houses for the staff. The houses were rent free for life and disinfected every other day. There were changing rooms for the staff and visitors next to the reception area of the Hos-Spit-Hall. The staff changed into made-to-measure uniforms made from recycled paper which were burnt after use each day. Visitors were scrubbed down before entering the area and given recycled paper boiler suits to wear. This cut the number of visitors to a trickle, saving the staff a lot of time and trouble.

Dunsay saw Sam's eyes water at the news. She told him she would miss him and wished him a speedy return to full health. She fell asleep exhausted after all she had seen and done.

The party of Beatles were boarding in India when she awoke. She could not believe the change in them. They had all grown long beards and looked completely different, wearing what looked like white dresses down to their ankles with strings of beads around their necks and flowers in their unkempt hair.

Silla Blackfly herself and Septic Sam looked in awe and astonishment as they silently bowed their way on board, sat down and stared into some strange world in utter contentment. They were flying to the solitude of the Mull-Of-Kin-Cartney to meditate around the Ring-Go-Desire given to them with a rich smile by Guru Jappa Nogo. It was the size of a half-pound Beef Burger, a soft outer ring and a plywood centre gave it an aura of containing some strange elements. Made by the great man himself, he said if they believed strongly enough, it would drum them up a fortune of wealth and popularity. Dunsay could not help wondering if their brains had been cleansed in carbolic soap or something.

Dunsay awoke in the morning in her cosy, warm bed feeling tired and hungry. She could not believe it had all been a dream. The whole incredible journey was so clear in her mind. At breakfast, Mum scolded her for scoffing her food down as if she had not eaten for a month. Later, as they were all being weighed, Bargan could not believe her eyes. Dunsay had lost four pounds in weight overnight. Dunsay was not surprised, maybe one day Mum would believe in the Dream Maker.

HELPFUL
ADVICE
TO
YOUNGER
GENERATIONS

As an eighty years old male heading nearer towards my departure, some advice and helpful hints to digest for younger generations. As a teenager going out to rock and roll the night away, an elderly gentleman gave some sound advice, we took no heed, regrets were to follow.

In your years of youth, vitality, enthusiasm and extreme hormonal arousal, think before you speak or act rashly. One sexual act on impulse or bad temper strike can change your life forever.

In a humane way children need a measure of discipline and order in their upbringing. In my childhood the Tawse, a leather strap cut into strips at the receiving end of your outstretched hand was used in Scotland's schools. Teachers and parents working in collaboration. Although this did us more good than harm, today's methods are more civilised. An example of why discipline from an early age is important. With the sudden freedom the rock and roll era gave us, it took National Service of two years, beginning with eight weeks marching, rifle drill, with large amounts of humiliation to dampen our cocky attitudes.

To be self-sufficient and independent are more than rewarding in the long run. Granny and Grandad, Mummy and Daddy, will not be around forever. Remember we come into this world with nothing and depart in the same way.

Boredom is a health hazard, so be creative for a fuller social life. Mixing with people from all walks of life is an education in itself. Envy is soul-destroying. Ambition within the bounds of contentment with your lot is a blessing. It takes patience and dedication to expand on your potential.

Never say never.

Keep the loan sharks from your door by living within your means. Save your pennies to appreciate the pounds. If you have spare cash, invest some in a few well-known brand names, on the stock market. Do not rush in, but study their ups and downs. Try buying when times are hard and shares are low. Patience is the name of the game. From Saga, Sales Direct and others, information flows. In time, your outlay, dividends will cover. Buy some Premium Bonds, it is money you can forget about until an emergency happens. You might even strike lucky and hit a jackpot without losing a penny.

Your conscience and daily problems produce the silent killer called stress. With carefree holidays or week-end breaks give them a rest. Do not swap these for material items, the house extension, new settee etc. These create tension and can wait. 'I WANT IT NOW' is a NO, NO.

Cooking your own soups, stews and veg stop wrinkles up the face to spread and will save you pounds. It is all good news, helps tummy shrink and not protrude.

Count your blessings when down or depressed, for millions would love your lifestyle, who have not even a bed. Dump the junk food, keep body in trim, a few years I have no doubt you will win.

With our past and present history, taking into account we are supposed to be the most intelligent species on earth, how in heaven's name can we think we are entitled to an afterlife.

When you get to my age it is a great morale booster to think the impossible, that you will live
FOREVER.

With that thought in mind I am content with my life.

WILLS

It is important to update your Will when necessary. After a number of years you can usually do this for free. Contact your solicitor for information. The age of full maturity of most adults in my opinion is mid twenties for females and late twenties for males. Sorry gentlemen, but I am trying to be honest. Where large amounts of wealth is involved it should be held in trust with provisos if the client has misgivings about the recipients.

To avoid family squabbles after your demise, even though you are past caring, do not leave any close relations out of your Will. After the tears (wishful thinking) over your departure this can result in costly court proceedings contesting your Will and family splits, or maybe one or two entertaining punch-ups. Leaving a little for the disgruntled means more for the jollier. Let it go, you have nothing more to lose.

A legacy that will stand the test of time in word, song or good deed can give the Will maker satisfaction and peace of mind. Bill Gates I am sure would agree. Many marriages and partnerships do not turn out to be happy ever after. Love can become extremely nasty and expensive. I have been there.

A pre-nuptial agreement is advisable with security for both parties and children, if involved. Mortgage hikes trap the unwary.

THE TAWSE

In Scottish schools
it reigned supreme
for many generations.
Of leather made
two inches wide
the hand and wrist
with might did find.
Cut into strips
at the receiving end
red weals of discipline
was Tawse's aim.
Five years old
a tiny mite
in front of class
he stood,
for peeing against
the wall of school
was now about
to pay in full.
The Tawse came down
six times in all
made hand swell
he wanted to bawl,
but with his pride
now at stake

unflinching he stared ahead.
The Tawse was law and order
teachers with parents
in control, of offsprings
who stepped out of line
made to do
what they were told.

LOVE ROMANTICA

There is a well-known saying, 'It is better to have loved and lost than never to have loved at all.' Most songs are also linked to romantic love such as, 'Love is a many-splendoured thing.'

This may be so, but it can also be a recipe for disaster, as millions of divorcees, battered wives and husbands and the anguish suffered by families as a whole, can testify to. It is also responsible for countless suicides.

Romantic love is a potent chemistry between two people that can devour common sense, decency, and free speech.

It is a sad fact that most people have to reach the wisdom of old age, to experience the merits of solitude, contemplation and contentment with one's lot, if good health permits.

DIVORCE

It breaks the bond
of all involved
as papers served
on marriage cold.
All branches of
the family tree
axed with a finality
no longer stable
on emotion road
when shedding of
the family code.

Modern Times is a compilation of poetry, featuring some of our finest poets. The book gives an insight into the essence of modern living and deals with the reality of life today. We think we have created an anthology with universal appeal.

There are many technical aspects to the writing of poetry and *Modern Times* contains free verse and examples of more structured work from a wealth of talented poets. To choose winners from the wide range of styles and forms is a most difficult task, albeit a pleasurable one. On this occasion, the winners are as follows.

Mr R Fallon	Torment Of The Ring
Hazel Houldey	Berlin Wall
Paddy Jupp	September Days

My congratulations and thanks go to them and to all of you who have contributed to *Modern Times,* and I trust you will enjoy it as much as I have.

TORMENT OF THE RING

Looking back it was never meant to last
The flirtatious nature of her spirit
Was imprisoned by the band of gold
Pressed on her by pregnancy.
The childlike insistence on matrimonial tradition
Taking no heed of his limited resources,
Or her condition
Sent alarm bells ringing.
Surprisingly she had a flair for motherhood
From those precious baby stages,
Attentive, caring almost doting.
It was he who lacked words if not deeds
The sentiments to give her
A more secure awareness of his presence.
The financial struggle to establish themselves
Bound them together.
At last free of child care
With city job carefully chosen
The opportunity for flattery and adulation
Her ego craved.
Nights out with the girls became more frequent
Home coming later, excuses more trivial,

Encouragement to socialise on his own.
Her breathless excitement, flushed face
On more than one late excursion
Reminded him of a summer evening
Wrestling playfully on flattened hay
Her thin cotton dress rucked high.
Jealousy and suspicion were now ripe
He knew he was being taken for a fool
The marriage was as good as over.
Tight lipped he refused to question
Afraid of the truth, his pride still intact.
Self doubt also festered
Would a daily show of adoration
With a weekly bunch of roses
Have sufficed to keep her on track.
Too late, he would never know
On table a note topped by her band of gold
Left her torment behind.

TEENY LOVE

My eyes are streaming
From tears are stung
You've left me for
Another one.
Mary Bell is her name
You told her lies
To stake a claim.
Said that I cheated on you
With a boy called Johnny Blue.
She knows of our foreplay
Each secret you gave away.
Her claws are out
With tongue so sharp
Tells all and sundry
Of our romps in the park.
I walk downtown
To cat calls
'She pulled the plug on Bobby Hall'
In front of buddies
You feel real big
Exaggerate what I did
People think I'm no good at all
'She pulled the plug on Bobby Hall'

THE RUN

A life for two on bobsleigh
Warm in tandem they began.
The slope was steep
With skids now on
Till death do part
Not their swan song.
Fighting, bickering, jealousy,
They fought it hard along the way
Steering straight was hard to do.
Into bends at breakneck speed
A crash was on the cards
Finally reached the finishing line
Bodies battered, weary in mind.
Bobbing with the joy and strife
Such is life on a bobsleigh ride.

THE RIM

As tyre starts to thin
Only way headed is the rim
For human race alike
In circle life does go
Strong start to falter
As inner tubes blow,
Make most of tread
While in good trim
Satisfaction from life
You then will win.

SOMEONE ELSE IN BED

It should have been no surprise
The mess that he was in
Six months courting
Three months pregnant
Her mother hit the roof
With Daddy angry at the thought
Of his Blossom in full bloom.
They insisted on a white wedding
The wedding guests got merry
On his bank overdraft.
The first few years went quickly
Two daughters a year apart
Teaching them to walk then swim
Snowball fights in the park.
When girls reached age of puberty
He felt sort of shunned
They went all secretive
Talked only to their mum.
She got a part time city job
Made excuses to stay out late
At house-warmings and such.
One morning late for work
He answered the telephone
A male voice hesitated
Then asked is Lyn at home

She streaked downstairs
Voice flustered face bright red
He knew the time had come to ask
'Is someone else in bed?'

SLICK CHICK

Always takes centre stage
Classy dresser, raver too
Built to make men's pulses race
Wriggling, giggling full of fun
Until in wedlock he ends up
SLICK CHICK
Honeymoon now long past
Slick Chick in a spot of bother
Where's money gone from joint account?
She can't explain
Accuses him of being mean
Now hidden spite stored up in her
Aimed at him with screaming fit
SLICK CHICK
Starts to flirt with all and sundry
Till a toy boy she has captured.
Time for him to do a runner
Or be the doormat she is after.

LOVE'S TANGLED WEB

Compassion is love
To those with cross to bear
For others in oblivion
With dreams blank as they stare.
Relating love to close at heart
Great anguish felt when world depart
Consumes the mind to ultimate low
Until the wake of departed soul.
Love of power split a nation
White House was therapeutic patient.
Love also plays the heartstrings
Gives tears and joy in uneven tread.
Must have, don't count the cost
A sting in tail of love ill bought
A love child brings new meaning
With each genetic seed
For some blessing created
To others life-long grief.
Love can also turn to hate
Fill with vengeful thoughts
When love is dealt a double-cross.

To a one-night stand
Word can be stretched
Or a mile high club in a tight head.
But there is a love that's total
In body, mind and soul
Lifelong commitment
To make two become whole.

THREE IN ONE

At eighteen the world
Is her plaything
Whatever disguise
She may come in
Can manipulate the male hormone
Blush or brash can cause a storm,
At forty if kept in trim
She still reigns supreme
Security with love now mixed
In comfort zone
She finds her kicks.
At seventy has earned respect
For years of care of family set
No longer attracts with sex appeal
But can disarm with a smile.
There are exceptions to the rule
But why should I be kind or cruel.

ALTERNATIVE LIFESTYLE

Marriage over alternative was on
Bought little house with pub and job
Three minutes walk from home.
No more need for garden tools
Large park across the road
Where I can sit while lawns are cut
Concrete slabs round my abode,
Holidays abroad each year
My money now my own
I even eat when and what I want
And dress not as I'm told.
Cook and clean for myself
In case of a takeover.
For twenty years content I've been
Living as the wild rover,
I found myself a lady
To drive me to and from a drink
Young, virile and pretty
Pineapple juice she sips.
Now I'm getting on a bit
I might let her move in
To help me move my Zimmer Frame
When my old legs give in.

MORTALS

Burdened down with earthly sins
Who put them there not clear.
We rape, pillage, annihilate
Religion's name put to shame,
Concern about a life,
Hereafter
Makes our existence
A disaster.

THE PREACHERS

They come in different disguises
To enlighten, frighten and chastise
Read out Gospel from religious book.
Some speak of Brimstone and Damnation
Others of virgins in waiting.
Wise words written for our good
Used on weak-willed by the scheming.
A few in expensive business suits
With flashy wives, mansions build
Bought with money from converts
A couple in prison now domiciled.
For sexual perversions others go down
With blind eyes turned by their peers.
Some against equality of the sexes
Think only men can reach our senses.
Others with power gone to head
Think are immortal one on earth.
A lot of good some of them do
But safer to read and think for self.

THE SALVATION ARMY

The mightiest force known to man
Recruits of all nations in their ranks
It's battle banners stretch worldwide
Without a bloodstain on the mind.
The rank and file work night and day
Collecting for all charity.
Officers on paltry pay
Lead from front on missions grey
No bomb or bullet do they use
But with a news sheet air their views
If ever you are down and out
Soup, tea with bun, warm comfort shout
No preaching they of right or wrong
Or with the bible come on strong.
A bed in hostel will provide
With eggs and bacon sunny side.
When dying on life's battlefield
Always on hand to hold and shield
Your soul is safe within their ranks
All the world owe them thanks.

DIGNITY

In certain state of mind
For some the price is high,
Forever nose aimed at the sky
With downward stoop of eye.
In small amounts
It gives the scope
Pleasure in life to adopt,
But few get the balance right
To keep in check malicious spite.

From board game
marry-go-round
Old Bill involved
in marriage bliss.

LAW AND ORDER

A wedge between breakers
Of man made laws
And citizens of honesty.
Die for law
On mean streets
As on wrong doers
Put the heat.
Some sights
With which they deal
Churn the stomachs
Man and female.
A minority are as bent
As those they arrest.
To rig a statement
Not unknown.
Divorce rate high
Your wife might steal
We're only human
They then plead.
Some will cover
For a friend
Others will shop a brother.
A mixture of the human genes
Trying in honesty
To keep us clean.

DISCIPLINE
(BRITISH STYLE)

Ten-year-olds murdered
A little lad of two
Educated and pampered
Now in secret live as free.
Other kids running wild
Smoke, drink, sniff pots of glue.
Extortion by the bully
Now out of control
Of innocent heads, suicide roll call.
Elders live in fear and stress
Of the child they once held dear.
Threaten to smack a child of yours
Of social services beware.
The days have long gone
When punishment fitted the crime
And law and order was respected.

YOB AND STEAL SOCIETY
2011

Roll the joint, smoke the dope
Wrap my brains in overcoat
Drink the booze, lose control
Temper hits danger zone
Go on ecstasy, in a daze
Slavery from my own free will.
Take joy ride in someone's car.
No tax, insurance, what a laugh
Three best mates died in crash.
Six of us on to one
Put the boot in, play the thug
Grannies cower when they see us…
On a gang bang, hold the bird down
She asked for it, out late at night.
Scratch cars, set fire to schools
Break into property, then we trash
Steal anything on order sheet
Buyer waits with wad in fist.
We've taken over, now we rule
Parents now under our control.
If not show us enough respect
Bullet or Shaftin, you will get.

BRITAIN
2025

There was something eerily beautiful about the moon in winter as its light streaked through the trees, leaving large dark shadows. These were perfect cover for Jags Prescott as he waited impatiently in Sari Park on the outskirts of the multi-racial city of Leicester. It was the year 2025, like all retired people over the age of seventy-five part time working was compulsory. In the earlier years of the century, public confidence and patience with the three main political parties had finally run out. The native born population, angry at the way their wishes had long been ignored in favour of foreigners, who had put nothing into the national coffers, revolted. A bloodless revolution took place.

The nation was now run by an All Party Senate. Members were elected from all sections of the community by regional votes, for a three-year period on a fixed income. Anyone found fiddling the taxpayers was sentenced to ten years hard labour with no remission. All major decisions were decided by a National Referendum through the Internet. Human Rights law only applied to law-abiding citizens, anyone making unjust or stupid claims was fined and publicly humiliated. The dinosaur of political correctness was abolished. Voting on state affairs became compulsory from the age of sixteen. The House of Commons and the House of Lords plus Buckingham Palace, rid of all their wealthy trappings, became hard labour prisons for those serving a life sentence.

The All Party Senate served the nation from a derelict warehouse in Bradford, tastefully decorated with bankrupt stock wallpaper.

Within a year of the revolution the old and infirm were released from imprisonment in their own homes and could walk the streets without fear of attack. Muggers and young thugs didn't take kindly to the death sentence for attacking the vulnerable. Burglary became a thing of the past when life imprisonment with no remission and hard labour became law.

Prescott, long since retired, had been assigned to the Public Offenders Council Section. As he shivered in the cold night air he could not help envying his buddy, Tony Blair, who was studying the art of confidence trickery and coral density in Australia, with his wife, after retiring to the sun. With only squirrels for company he scanned the car park and bottle bank area twenty yards from his vantage point. His Byers van was safely hidden in some bushes. He thought back to the times of government incompetence and neglect of the law-abiding majority in favour of criminals and their do-gooder allies. Of Judges in a state of senility, way out of touch with reality. Industrial Tribunals for the working classes, chaired by people who acted like prosecutors with a demeaning attitude to claimants.

A figure appeared on the other side of the park. It was nearing curfew time for under sixteens. The youth relieved himself then zipped up his flies. Prescott clenched his fist in anger but let the offence go unpunished, hoping some dog-owner had taken a chance on his or her liberty and left some dog pooh for the lad to tread in. He was on surveillance for a set purpose, to apprehend or report a sighting of a criminal who had been a menace to the Senate for many years. Section helpers were on watch in prime target areas of the city, after intelligence reports of this public enemy number one. Crime had increased from zero to one third of a hundred percent over the last five years. Maybe it was time for a referendum on stiffer sentences.

As he scanned the area behind him with powerful night sights, supplied for this job, he saw movements in the darkening shadows.

He gave way to a moment of panic, there were strange wild creatures on the loose all over the country. Three of these interbreeds had been around for a long time, nibbling away at the country's wealth, undetected by most of the population. The Labourstrikeforus, Liberalhomo and Toriaboris were as great a danger to themselves as the rest of the country. When cornered, their snapping, backbiting and infighting was stomach-churning. In the year 2006 Animal Rights activists had freed thousands of animals all over the country.

Large numbers of these laboratory experiments had survived in the wild. Over the years they interbred into bizarre and sometimes dangerous life forms. The government of the time did not help by banning Fox hunting, making them more or less an endangered species. The Fox population grew out of control and interbred with, among others, vicious Alsatians, released on striking miners by their angry police handlers. Racing Whippets who their striking owners could not afford to feed during the violent, Thatch Head Scargill era of the late nineteen hundreds, when the whole country was undermined. This led to a fearsome hybrid named the Alwhipafox. The creature was agile, cunning and savage, with an acquired taste for human flesh.

As they hunted in packs from dusk till dawn, Jags Prescott had good reason to be concerned. A part time government busybody and sleep inducer, credited as the creator of the Brazil Wax, unselfishly gave his all to try and exterminate the Alwhipafox. Professor Mandelson took out second mortgages on his homes to finance research into the production of a sleeping sickness drug, which at one stage nearly succeeded in wiping out the Alwhipafox. The survivors, due to their devious nature, made a remarkable comeback against all the odds, they became a law unto themselves.

With the demise of the railways after a permanent strike by angry and disgruntled passengers, the Alwhipafox foraged from their railway sleeper dens and abandoned sidings at will, with all the other hybrids including the giant headed Mink Skinner Otter, a human-induced catastrophe.

The railways had been replaced by intercity robot driven carriages named Byers, after the man responsible for their manufacture. Powered by magnetic propulsion on a single rail, they were pollution free and easily accessible from the magnetic propelled pavements and boardwalks. With the decrease in the use of petrol and diesel driven vehicles, two lanes of all motorways were re-turfed as reclaimed green belt. A green belt stake rush ensued, led by itinerant travellers.

The caravan swelling population increased by the thousands overnight. Councils went into the red as millions of pounds were lost in council tax and the housing market collapsed. Ministers faced a House of Commons enquiry and had their hands slapped.

As he kept his lonely vigil, Prescott thought of the state of lawlessness and mass immigration that had taken place before the Revolution. As the thin blue line of law and order dispersed in large numbers to the coasts, to repel the swarms of illegal immigrants, law and order was in a traffic jam. Sari Park became a squatter camp for thugs, drug dealers and joy riders. Cars stolen by kids as young as ten were set on fire for the sheer hell of it. The area had also fostered it's fair share of teenage unmarried mothers, chain smoking impatiently during their career move, a top of the list, three-bedroomed council house. Smoking the weed was now a criminal offence, under age addicts served six months in a tented boot camp on a stable diet of cold turkey. If they re-offended they faced three years in prison with their parents and repeated showings of televisions Big Brother as their only entertainment.

Hard drugs were prohibited unless on prescription, illegal drug use meant life imprisonment. Drug dealers were not so lucky, they served two years as guinea pigs in a scientific experimental unit. If they survived they could look forward to death by lethal injection. Prescription drugs were only obtainable from Senate hospitals, patrolled by armed guards.

Parental centres housed neighbours from hell where they were taught basic morals and sterilised. The old fashioned ideology that children should be seen and not heard made a startling comeback.

The opening of non-profit Senate shops in towns and villages had reversed shopping trends. The out of town supermarkets could no longer compete and leased their premises to the Senate, who turned them into Litter Lout centres and Inter Space holiday departure and arrival points. Litter offenders spent eight hours a day for a week on pick it up, bin it courses, knee-high in an acre of the now banned junk mail and plastic bags.

Second offenders were sent to landfill rubbish sites on three months dig it up, re-bury it digs. There was no third time offender on record. The countryside also benefited from a minimum sentence of ten years for illegal dumping of rubbish. Most of the prisons had been closed because for some reason people didn't seem to want to go there anymore.

The Moon was now home to a gigantic domed holiday complex, devoid of time-share reps. It was built as a replica to all the tiny parts of life over the last hundred years that were actually pleasant in between the almost continuous wars, torture, starvation and suffering of the world's vast majority. The old fashioned holidays with knees in the chest flying had taken a back seat. The huge Inter Space Rockets had full-length reclining seats, with walkabouts for star and space viewing, plus all modern facilities for three hundred passengers. They were powered by a weightless fuel named Trolly Titanium, which was invented by Neil Kincockup who awoke one morning with his head in a spin. After much trial and error it was eventually refined in Iran and renamed National Hell Supplement, or N.H.S. for short. Inter Space holidays were on a rota basis, anyone with a criminal or dubious terrorist record was banned from travelling anywhere for life.

An owl startled Jags Prescott out of his dream holiday mood as it swooped on its prey near the Park playing field. He stamped his feet as the cold began to bite into his Chinese boots and clothing.

Three super powers now existed, their currency now known as the Yankee Obama, the Chinese Triad and last but not least the Indian In-got. Euroland could not compete with each giant expanding colony and was swallowed up. With a new-found freedom to travel a flood of Chinese made their way to enter easy Britain. Their destination was France, to enjoy a massive baby boom outside their strict birth control homeland, a refined health service, large pensions and the freedom to strike or disrupt without the fear of prosecution. France in desperation dynamited their end of the Channel Tunnel to stem the flow of illegal Chinese and others from Britain.

France cut it's Human Rights law to the bone as their treasury was raided by frivolous complaints from the illegal and criminals. In fear of complete domination by China and fearful of American friendly fire, Euroland became, with England, a part of the United States of India. Scotland and Wales remained Independent, as they had been for many years. Before gaining independence from England, the Scottish Parliament reversed or changed many decisions made by the British Parliament in London, which strange as it may seem, was led by a group of Scots. When the Scottish Parliament introduced free university education, improved and cheaper care for their elderly plus many other benefits, people in England became a little upset.

Many poor and middle class white English and Muslims made a permanent move to Scotland. Their glowing reports of life in the north attracted so many more in the south that the Scots were forced into rebuilding the whole of the Roman Empires Hadrians Wall to keep them out. Scotland finally gained full Independence under the banner of the Scottish National and Muslim Party.

Meanwhile in the south, English parents were sending their daughters to Bollywood dancing classes in the hope that they would catch the eye, in their perma-tan and sari, of a rich man with marriage in mind. With their lower birth rate and mixed marriages the white English population was now a minority.

In Wales a Welsh child singer had progressed into a television personality and from that into politics. She became the first female Prime Minister of her country. A song was written in her honour, with the title, 'Rugby, Bubbly and Church,' it was sung to the tune of 'Land of My Fathers.' The first law passed under the leadership of Prime Minister Church stated that no foreigner would be allowed to buy property in Wales or stay for more than six weeks, apart from Welsh exiles with holiday homes.

Wales became the last country in the whole of Europe to be ruled wholly by its own nationals. America had taken it for granted that England, their closest ally, would eventually join them as another state.

This dream was destroyed by the collapse of the American housing market in 2008. This caused a chain reaction around the world, bringing untold hardship and misery. A case of friendly fire from greedy Bankers. Americas reluctance to lead from the front in the fight against Global Warming had also done nothing to enhance its reputation. It was shaken out of its complacency a few years later. A Chinese corporation succeeded in a takeover bid for America's worldwide food suppliers. Macdonalds, Beef Burger King and Kentucky Fried Chicken were dissolved into the 'Melting Pots'. This was after obesity had spread around the globe like a cancer and people were dying in their thousands from gas inhalation. The 'Melting Pots' served a variety of quality foods and chopsticks gave their customers some much-needed exercise. Their most popular dishes were 'Doodle While You Noodle', 'Doodle While You Dunk', 'Chopstick Duet', 'Yankee Doodle Jammy', 'Dragon Fire My Bite', Milk Rattle and Roll' and the chefs surprise 'Text Till You Retch'.

The 'Melting Pots' restaurants-cum-kindergartens became national institutions teaching racial harmony, respect and protection for all life forms and the environment, with their pleasantly illustrated and anti-blasphemous Doodle books.

Jags Prescott was startled from his thoughts by the mournful sound of a siren from the vicinity of Mandela Park, on the other side of the city. Like many others he had been amazed that a man who spent the best part of his life in a cell, should have a park named after him that sat in the shadow of the towering wall of the city prison. The hair on the back of his bloated neck stiffened in alarm as he spotted a frail, stooped figure at the entrance to the Park, checking it out for what seemed like an eternity, before entering. With a shuffling gait the figure moved across the car park to the bottle bank, which had four holes for different coloured bottles. To his astonishment Prescott saw that the figure was carrying, with difficulty, three supermarket plastic bags, banned nearly two decades ago because of damage to wildlife and the environment.

The bags were filled to the brim and the shadowy figure reached the bottle bank with a weary sigh. Prescott pressed his microchip button to alert headquarters, before moving in for the kill. This person was committing what had been, in the days of political correctness, the most loathed crime, putting coloured bottles in the clear bottle hole. Even now this caused great confusion and anger when the multi-racial council workers opened the banks. The mixing of glass had also become the international symbol for the right to express ones thoughts freely without being accused of racism.

Prescott crept up on the suspect and challenged it. The figure turned slowly towards him. He felt weak at the knees when he saw whom he was about to arrest. It was none other than public enemy number one, Majestic Thatcher. When he regained his composure he helped the tottering Majestic to his Byers Van, with the little respect he could muster. With his prisoner safely in the van, his chest swelled with pride as he thought of the rewards and publicity he would get from his arrest.

Reality hit him like a hammer blow. Behind him he heard a savage snarling that tailed off into a whippet-like whine, which chilled him to the marrow. With his bodily functions running out of control, he turned to face the pointed fangs of the Alwhipafox.

Prescott's last shift was nearly over.

WILLIAM SHAKESPEARE

Will our master
Of the word
With each phrase
The mind to stir.
Through War and Peace
Your works live on
To feed each intellect
Weak or strong.
Shylock on to Macbeth,
Greed, lighthearted
To great depth.
Romeo with Juliet
Bleeds the hearts
As tears still wept.
Stratford-on-Avon
Your monument
With house a shrine
To ink and pen.
Students all,
Who search to write,
Will Shakespeare read
Pen to enlight.